THE FLORIANS

A planetary colony is one life-system invading another. It's the seed of Earth trying to implant itself in alien soil. Of course the worlds have been surveyed, the life-systems inspected, and the whole venture certified practical by men who are trained to guess right.

But it's not as simple as that. When a life-system in balance is invaded by another, there are bound to be ecological repercussions, both short-term and long-term. The colonists have no way of analysing the ecological effects of their invasion, let alone any capacity to mount a long-range scientific programme to deal with them. Over a period of time there are bound to develop permanent antagonisms between the two life-systems. The invasion will cause permanent changes in *both* systems, as they react to one another and, in the long term, adapt to one another.

The *Daedalus* was designed to re-contact colonies. It's a flying laboratory, fitted out for the specific tasks of genetic analysis and genetic engineering. Its job is to help resolve the antagonisms which inevitably develop between the life-systems.

'THE FLORIANS' is the thrilling novel of its first planetary mission.

Brian M. Stableford

THE
FLORIANS

Hamlyn Paperbacks

THE FLORIANS
ISBN 0 600 33668 9

First published in Great Britain 1978
by Hamlyn Paperbacks
Copyright © 1976 by Brian M. Stableford

Hamlyn Paperbacks are published by
The Hamlyn Publishing Group Ltd,
Astronaut House,
Feltham,
Middlesex, England

Made and printed in Great Britain
by Cox & Wyman Ltd,
London, Reading and Fakenham

PROLOGUE

It was late September, the trees shedding their useless leaves, stripping down for the winter with the aid of a hurried, anxious wind. A man and a boy were walking along the river bank. The river was dark and turbid, and despite the waves fluttering its surface it seemed heavy and sluggish. The banks on either side, where the frail trees still eked out their lives despite the shadows which hid them from the sun for most of the day, were flanked with high, smooth faces of concrete. The living city, where windowed buildings blossomed from the roofs of the labyrinthine catacombs, was high in the sky. Its sounds filtered down into the deep crack where the river ran, but they were distant, muted. The place where the man walked with his son was part of an older, forgotten world: a world where privacy remained.

The man wore a coat, and his hands were buried in his pockets as he cowered from the chilly gusts. His head was held at an angle, turned away from the dust which the wind picked up and threatened to hurl into his eyes. The boy was more lightly dressed, but he seemed accustomed to the wind, oblivious to its hostilities. He walked with a lighter step, but slowly – as though uncertain of his direction.

The man had just passed forty, the age at which – by the tradition of common parlance – life may begin again, changing direction and entering a new phase. The boy was stranded in the ambiguous years between youth and maturity – perhaps seventeen, or a year to either side. They were both tall, lanky, dark haired. The man wore a heavy tan – the legacy of time recently spent in the tropics, which had not had time to fade. The boy, beside him, seemed unnaturally pale of skin.

They were talking, one to another, but an interested

observer might have noted the way that their eyes flickered from side to side, and the fact that they always walked slightly apart. Despite their blood relationship, they seemed to be strangers, lost in the desert of their conversation, unable to meet and exchange any real confidence. They did not know what to say, or how.

'I'm sorry there isn't more time,' said the man. His name was Alexis Alexander. His son's name was Peter. 'The schedule is tight. And the operation . . . well, it isn't exactly secret, but there's to be no publicity. The political situation . . . you know better than I . . . it's delicate.'

'Slipping quietly away into the depths of space,' said the boy. 'Behind the nation's back.'

'It's nothing to do with the nation,' said the man. 'It's the whole world.'

'Behind *all* the nations' backs,' amended the boy.

They said more with the manner of their speaking than with the words they used. The man was reluctantly defensive. He chose his words carefully, not because he was undecided in his thoughts, but because he knew that what he said was offensive to the boy. The boy was doubtful and unhappy. He was also resentful – determined to place the responsibility for his doubt and unhappiness on his father's shoulders.

'You know that I believe in this,' said the man. 'I've worked for it all my life. I believe that this is something which must be done, for historical as well as moral reasons. All my life I've wanted the chance I have now. Please try to understand that.'

'I don't understand,' said the boy. 'I can't understand how anyone can condone – let alone participate in – such a criminal waste of effort, of resources, of money. What's the purpose of history if we can't and won't learn from our mistakes? When the last starship carried colonists into space seventy-five years ago the Earth was in ruins. Seven billion people were left with the wreck of a world which had used up everything it had to send seven million people to alien planets. For every man that went out, a thousand were left behind. And for every dollar spent on the men who stayed, a thousand were spent on the ones who left. And yet it took years of fighting, civil war endemic over ninety per cent of the globe, to get the lunacy stopped. Now you – and people like you – want to start it all again. You want to bring back the space age. You want to bring back the world where people's needs were met with hopeless dreams. Even in seventy-five years, we haven't *begun* to sort out the problems which the human race faces here on Earth, and you want to put the clock back, to forget all the real problems and put all our efforts into denying a thousand men so that one can take a crazy chance in space. What's the use of a new world – a hundred new worlds – when we can't even look after the one we've got?'

The man picked up a loose stone from the earth beside the towpath, held it crooked between thumb and forefinger, and then sent it spinning out across the wave-flecked surface. It skipped once, twice, and then disappeared a foot or two short of the opposite bank. The waves scurrying upstream against the current hungrily absorbed the ripples which spread out from each point of contact.

'There'll always be problems on Earth,' said the man simply. He didn't want to argue.

'But we don't always have to turn our backs on them.'

'We can't wait for Utopia,' said the man. 'It's like tomorrow – forever in the future.'

The boy resented the lightness of the remark, but he relaxed nevertheless. He let a few seconds pass by, while the wind drained the tension from the air. Then, in a quiet voice, he said, 'Where did the money come from?'

The man almost smiled. He made a sound halfway between a cough and a laugh. 'It came in. Covertly. We didn't get any vast handouts. No government voted us a share of its gross national product. But the UN has some first-class beggars. It was borrowed, stolen, extorted . . . whatever you care to call it. I don't know how it shows up in the books when governments publish their accounts. Long-term investment, research, contribution to international project work – there are a million euphemisms to excuse the way taxpayers' money is spent. It took years, mind you, to get the

7

Daedalus fitted out, and more years while it sat idle until they could pay for its first run. There were scandals, but over the years these things get forgotten. There was no big splash when the ship came back after the first run, and there'll be no big splash when she takes off again. It's not secret – it's just that the story's been dragged out so long people are past caring.'

'That's not true,' said the boy, with a bitterness in his voice which made it clear that it *was* true. 'There are people who care. There are people who'd like to blow that ship to kingdom come if they could only get to it. You know what they call you ... the men who ride that ship? Ratcatchers. That's what they say you are – interplanetary ratcatchers.'

The man smiled bleakly.

'I know,' he replied. 'And it's true. We're ratcatchers. Only I don't take the word as an insult. It needn't be said in a derisory way. There are nicer ways of describing our mission, but ratcatcher is good enough for me. Do you know *why* they call us ratcatchers?'

'Because that's what you do,' said the boy. 'You contact all the old colonies – the ones that were set up a couple of hundred years ago. And you clear out their vermin. Because that's all that you *can* do.'

The man nodded. 'That's the trouble with a no-publicity policy,' he said. 'You can't keep secrets, so people get to know anyhow, but they get the vulgarised version. Well ... OK. We recontact the colonies, we offer them help, and the only help that's easy to offer is know-how. Scientific know-how. We ask them what sort of problems they have, and we try to help them solve the problems. If they have problems with vermin, we find them a way to exterminate the vermin. So we're ratcatchers.

'But you have to realise that that's the kind of problems the colonies *do* have. You have to remember that the old colony ships were built for the purpose of transporting as many people as possible from point A to point B. The ships were giant tin cans, with humans packed into them like sardines. The colonies started with virtually nothing in the way of resources. No continual contact with Earth was possible –

it's easy and cheap to build big ships that lift once and land once, but it's next to impossible to finance ships like *Daedalus* which can go in and out of gravity holes more or less at will. The colonies we're recontacting now have been out of touch with Earth for at least a century; some of them were never contacted at all, but just left to get on with things. The colony worlds had been passed as habitable, the colonists were given the barest elements of a civilisation, and that was *it*. They had to start in on their new worlds with very little else but bare hands. Now, three or four or seven generations later, we go back to them. What's the most important thing we can take them? What's the thing that they need most?

'We can no more send them equipment now than we could when they first went out. We can't take them anything material at all. So we take them the means to find answers to their problems. Individual colonies have individual problems, but we know damn well that they all have one general *class* of problems to face, and that's the class of *problems of co-adaptation*.

'A colony is one life-system invading another. It's the seed of Earth trying to implant itself in alien soil. Sure, the worlds have been surveyed, the life-systems inspected, and the whole venture certified practical by men who are trained to guess and guess right. But it's not as simple as that. When a life-system in balance is invaded by another there are bound to be ecological repercussions, both short-term and long-term. The colonists have no way of analysing the ecological effects of their invasion, let alone any capacity to mount a long-range scientific programme to deal with them. Most problems can be dealt with at a superficial level – treatment of the symptoms, as you might say – but over a period of time there are bound to be permanent antagonisms developed between the two life-systems. The invasion will cause permanent changes in *both* systems, as they react to one another and – in the long term – *adapt* to one another.

'The *Daedalus* was designed to recontact colonies. It was built with the assumption that such colonies would, by now, be established to a certain degree. They would be technologically primitive even with a large reservoir of knowledge and information to draw upon. And they would be engaged in a constant battle with the alien life-system: a battle which had, itself, become a way of life. The purpose of the *Daedalus* is to help such colonies win such battles. It's a flying laboratory, fitted out for the specific tasks of genetic analysis and genetic engineering. Its job is to help resolve the antagonisms which inevitably develop between the life-systems. At a crude level, the means which the alien life-system evolves to attack the invading life-system have to be neutralised, and that's what the recontact mission is for. According to the vulgar metaphor, it's a matter of catching alien rats. Fair enough – the rats have to be caught.'

'I see,' said the boy flatly.

'It's necessary,' said the man, trying very hard to make his point. 'Without such help, colonies may die. You complain about the waste of effort putting them there. But wouldn't the *real* waste be leaving them to die? Even if it was wrong to send the colony ships out – and I can't agree even with that – surely it can't be wrong to do what we have to in order to give them a reasonable chance of success. We're *committed* now. We have to be.'

The boy stared steadfastly forward, watching the river as it flowed into the narrow crack that was the faraway horizon of the concrete walls. Though parallel, the walls did not appear to meet at infinity. There was a thin sliver of sky, out beyond the city's boundary.

'You don't have to convince me,' said the boy. 'It's nothing to do with me. You've never pretended to be any different. You're an ecologist ... all your life you've been involved in experiments with alien plants brought to Earth in the old days ... that and trying to figure out how to help Earth's life-system survive the rape that the human race has subjected it to these last few hundred years. This *Daedalus* thing is made for you. It's the perfect opportunity for you to use your ability and your training. You don't need to justify yourself to me.'

'But you hate me for it,' said the man, the worlds slipping from momentarily unguarded lips.

'No,' said the boy. 'Why should I?'

The man could find nothing to say for a few moments. When he began again it was a return to safer ground.

'The first run proved the thinking right,' he said, in a low, patient voice. 'Of the five worlds contacted, four had the kind of problem the *Daedalus* personnel could attack in the lab. The rats were caught – and you can't underestimate the significance of that. Those colonies were helped.'

'And what about the fifth?'

The man looked away, his gaze flickering across the water to the far bank, and on up the concrete face to the heights where the grimy windows gleamed with reflected light. He continued to scan the arrays of glass panes, as though trying to imagine the myriad private lives concealed behind them.

'The fifth colony had already failed,' the boy accused.

'The ship was too late,' said the man. 'The political climate didn't improve fast enough for them. Mother Earth spent too long searching her pockets for the loose change.'

'Thousands of people,' said the boy. 'They shipped out with promises of a garden of Eden. Out of the cesspit into the grave. A children's crusade. In pursuit of a crazy dream. Was it really worth it?'

'They could have succeeded.'

'Could they?'

'If help had come sooner.'

'And what about the people here?' asked the boy. 'Billions of people. Facing the third great plague. Facing starvation. Facing foul water and poisoned air. Who'd have helped them if all the money was spent on flying laboratories to help the colonies? Your ship may save thousands of lives. You and your mission may work wonders out there in space. But how many lives could the same money save right here? Even in this country – this city – where, by the grace of God, things are supposed to be going just great ... what *was* yesterday's death toll, incidentally?'

The man would only shake his head.

Again, the argument died. Again, the anger and the anguish blew away with the dust. They both let it go. Neither wanted to spend the minutes that were ticking away in accusations, in recriminations, in ideological squabbling.

11

They both knew that there could be no possible gain. But they seemed to find little that they held in common save for the mutual antagonism.

It was all more in sorrow than in anger. But they could find no way out of the trap.

'You have your dreams all mixed up with your idea of reality,' said the boy.

'Don't we all?' the man replied.

'It seems to me,' said the boy, 'that you have something of a problem in co-adaptation right there.'

There was no laughter.

'The mission will solve it,' declared the man.

'And suppose it doesn't?'

The man shrugged the question away. It seemed nonsensical. But his son repeated it.

'Visiting the colonies isn't going to change my mind,' said the man. 'How could it?'

'I don't know,' said the other, 'but where there's life, there's hope.'

'If you want to trade platitudes,' said the man, 'how about: "We're all in the gutter, but some of us are looking at the stars"?'

'Great,' said the boy. 'Trouble is, the stars are all that you see. Look down here occasionally, and take a good look at the gutter we're in. Looking at the stars doesn't help to get it cleaned up.'

The man flinched from a blast of wind.

'What do you *want* me to do?' he asked baldly.

The boy chose his words very carefully. 'I don't think I really care,' he said. It was a plain statement, unalleviated by any hint of doubt in the tone. But the silence that fell obviously embarrassed him. He felt the need to supplement the declaration with some kind of explanation – some kind of excuse.

'Your sense of values is upside down,' he said. 'All your life you've been more interested in the Extraterrestrial than the Terrestrial. You've never been off the Earth but you've never really lived on it, either. You've worked for the UN on ecological problems right here – projects on which millions of lives might depend – but I've never seen you emotionally involved with a single one. You treat them all as purely theoretical exercises. In your letters you talk about experiments and observations as things in themselves, devoid of any meaning in human terms. You don't seem to realise what a wreck of a world this is.

'In three thousand years of human history we've destroyed our planet. We haven't conquered disease or starvation or misery with our ongoing technological revolution ... in fact, we haven't got *anything* in return for the destruction and the devastation. And yet we talk about second chances for humanity, about the conquest of the star-worlds. Why? What's the second chance *for* except to do it all over again, to wreck more worlds, to fill more open sewers with miserable humanity?'

The man stopped to skim another stone. It skipped three times and made it on to the path which ran along the far bank.

'You think in slogans,' he said. 'I know you're young, and you see things in extremes, but what you've said isn't anything like the truth, and you must know it. Of course we don't have Utopia, and we don't look forward to making or finding Utopia. People do starve, and die, and we don't have control over our use of the world's resources because demand is far, far greater than the poor old Earth can supply. All the platitudes which you apply to the situation have emotional power: *Let's put our own house in order; Let's solve our problems at home instead of exporting them to the universe; Let's conquer one world before we ruin a hundred more.* But that's not the whole story. It doesn't even begin to put things in focus. It's too narrow-minded.'

'What we need,' said the boy, 'is narrower minds. Minds that aren't full of crap about the conquest of space and man's role in the universe and all the fantasies where people like to live because they can't stand it here.'

But the man wasn't listening now.

'It's really the wrong way around,' he mused. 'It should be the young who look ahead, into the future, and see possibilities instead of threats. It's the old who are orientated

13

backward in time, wondering about mistakes, trying to validate the past by maintaining the status quo. *You* should see the future in the stars instead of in the soil. *You* should believe in the colonies. If it were only a personal rebellion, it might be easier to figure, but you're the voice of your generation. Why? What have you got against dreams? But there's the ship, too, named for Daedalus when it was Icarus who wanted to fly as high as possible.'

'Icarus was punished for his presumption,' interrupted the boy.

'But our wings aren't made of wax and feathers,' said the man – still to himself rather than to his son. 'And in any case, the name has nothing to do with that particular myth. It's another classical joke. Daedalus was the first genetic engineer – the man who made the Minotaur . . . another exercise in co-adaptation, you see . . .'

'Forget it,' said the boy. 'Just forget it.' His weariness was deliberate, overacted.

The man wanted to find a way back to the beginning, thinking that if he could only start again it might somehow turn out a little better, a little easier. He hadn't come to argue, but to say goodbye. But there seemed no way it could be said without resentment, without rancour. He was going away, for six – perhaps seven – years. It was nothing new – he had been away for the greater part of the boy's life, but there is a profound difference between miles and light-years. Even seven years isn't forever, but it would be a far greater slice out of the boy's life than his own. And so the meeting . . . and the parting . . . were important, and difficult.

'They'll make a part of my salary available to you,' said the man. 'No strings. If you need it, take it.'

The boy was on the point of shaking his head, but apparently thought better of it. There was no point in refusing, to provoke more shallow and pointless argument. It was better to wait.

They reached a slit in the concrete face, where a long staircase ascended towards the living city. They began to climb. It was no longer possible to walk side by side. The boy went first. When they reached the top, the car was waiting.

'Can we give you a lift?' asked the man.

'No,' said the boy. 'It'd take you out of your way.'

It was on the tip of the man's tongue to insist, but he too let the moment pass. For once, they exchanged a lingering glance. There was a hint of guilt about it, on both sides. Neither could escape the suspicion that at some time in the indeterminate future they might regret that this parting had passed so emptily, without any real feeling on either side – a formality.

In truth, they were being honest now in revealing no depths of emotion, maintaining an easy distance from one another. It would be in the future, with the creeping regrets and the notions of what *ought* to have been, that hypocrisy would cover up the reality.

They had nothing in common. In spite of heredity, it is often the way.

They shook hands, mouthed meaningless sounds, and parted. The son, consumed by the affairs of life and immediate circumstance, walked away into the city. The father, in getting into the car, cut himself out from that complex pattern, and headed for the stars.

'It was difficult?' said Pietrasante.

'He doesn't understand,' Alexander replied. 'He hasn't much sympathy with viewpoints other than his own.'

'He's a neo-Christian, isn't he?'

Alexander, who had let the acceleration of the car ease him back into the soft seat, felt a sudden tightness in his muscles.

'It's not illegal,' he said.

Pietrasante smiled. 'No need to be so touchy, Alex,' he purred. 'No need at all. I approve of the things the neo-Christians stand for; the refusal to yield to violence ... the utter rejection of violence as a means of human intercourse ... turning the other cheek. Of course, the violence they abhor is sometimes the violence of the establishment. They clash with authority ... but we need the kind of determination the neo-Christians show. There are too many people who find violence too easy to tolerate.'

'They're Monadists as well as Christians,' said Alexander. 'They don't want the space age back. If they found out where the *Daedalus* is they'd be lying underneath her daring us to take off over their dead bodies. As far as Peter is concerned, that's what I'm doing ... going to the stars over his dead body. He wouldn't lift a finger to stop me, of course, because he's a neo-Christian. But that's what he thinks.'

'That's the strength of the movement,' said Pietrasante. 'They don't stop anyone doing anything. They stand before the barrel of the gun, and they say "Shoot." And people don't ... sometimes. Most men with guns need an excuse to shoot, inside themselves. Even a petty criminal shooting an unarmed man in order to rob him needs to see his victim as an enemy, and himself as a potential victim. The neo-Christians, by attacking that assumption, are making the first constructive move against the socialisation of violence that our poor little planet has seen in many years.'

'And a lot of them get shot,' said Alexander quietly. 'Martyrs to the cause. Maybe the guys who kill them feel guilty as hell about it afterwards, but they're still dead. Dying for all mankind, they reckon, like Christ himself. But dying.'

'You think that may happen to your son?'

'Yes. I'm afraid that when I come back, in six or seven or ten years, I'm going to find Peter six feet under, because he stood in front of a gun and expressed his willingness to be shot. . . . I don't have the same confidence in the conscience of gunmen that you seem to have.'

'Would it make any difference,' asked the UN man quietly, 'if you were here when it happened?'

'No,' said Alexander. 'None at all.'

Pietrasante allowed a few minutes to pass, while he stared over the shoulder of the driver at the road ahead. Alexander looked sideways, his eyes not really focusing, letting the world become a blur as it whipped past the fast-moving car.

When the two men looked at one another again, they were ready to change gear, to turn their attention to problems of an entirely different order.

Pietrasante was carrying a number of files, which the

other man had returned to him before the meeting with his son. Now he tapped the files with a stout forefinger, and said, 'What do you think of Dr Kilner's observations?'

'How is Kilner?' countered Alexander.

'Still active,' said Pietrasante smoothly. 'He wasn't drummed out of the service. He's in charge of a reclamation project.'

'The Sahara?'

'Farther east.' Pietrasante flashed a tiny smile as he said it. Alexander did not return it.

'You couldn't expect him to be pleased by what he found,' said Alexander. 'Five colonies – four making a somewhat precarious living, one dead. Kilner believed in the colonies. He went out looking to find healthy societies, expanding populations, happy people. Instead, he found people ready to spit in his face because they thought they'd been deserted, left to rot. He couldn't live with the fact that they'd lost faith – that the contacts didn't renew their hope and re-vitalise the dreams the original colonists set out with. He had a hard time. And he despaired. Lost his own faith . . . became a convert to the antis. I think I understand – but I also think he was wrong. He *did* help those colonies. He *did* renew their hope, in a practical sense. He shouldn't have let their lack of gratitude get under his skin. It was no part of his job to be a hero. I still think he might have been all right if it hadn't been for the dead world. But that's what really knocked him down . . . it was too much, on top of everything else.'

'Suppose it had happened to you,' said Pietrasante.

Alexander looked the UN man full in the face, without any hesitancy in his manner. It was something he had not been able to do to his son. 'It may yet happen,' he said. 'I'm not going out wearing rose-tinted spectacles. If that's what Kilner found, that's what we'll find. I'm not going out there with the same optimism that he carried. I'm not searching for a new Arcadia. But I won't lose faith because I find the colonies struggling desperately to keep going and hating Earth because Earth has spent the best part of a century in a historical twilight zone when the whole space programme died. We have to start again, now. We have to look to the future.'

Pietrasante met the steady gaze with an expression of infinite calm. There was not the least sign of approval in his manner.

'Setting aside Kilner's personal reactions,' he said, 'what do you deduce from his reports on the individual worlds? Why were the colonies failing? In the beginning, each one was set up under the assumption that it would succeed even without further contact with Earth. All the volunteers were warned that no meaningful support might be possible for many years – even the two hundred years which have elapsed in the most extreme cases. The colonies were expected to survive in spite of that. Where did our thinking go wrong? Why were the colonies not the way Kilner expected to find them?'

Alexander, slightly resentful of the interrogation, turned away briefly. 'There was no single reason,' he said. 'Even in the case of the colony that failed, there was no single thing that we could point to and say, "*This* was the cause. *This* is what we had not anticipated." It's the whole class of problems – problems of co-adaptation between the life-systems. But these are problems which were bound to arise. And it's in the period of time which had elapsed in the recontacted colonies that we might have expected these problems to emerge and reach a critical point. I can't agree that the colonies Kilner helped would have failed utterly without him. They could have got past the crises on their own . . . things wouldn't have continued to get worse. Kilner saved lives and he saved time, but I believe that some of the colonies, at least, were viable in any case.'

'I'm not at all sure that I agree with you,' said Pietrasante. 'But my viewpoint is rather different from your own. Your interest is scientific, mine – I fear – has to be political as well. You see, these reports raise a good many questions with respect to the *Daedalus* project, and thus to the future of *any* new space programme. It is not simply a matter of deciding whether any new colonies are to be set up, or even what needs to be done about those already in existence . . . though these decisions have to be made, and Kilner's reports will be a powerful factor in influencing the decisions. There are more basic questions to be asked. Chief among them is this: Is the success or failure of any colony on any alien world primarily determined by biological factors or by social ones?

'As a biologist you are inclined to see the whole issue in terms of biological problems – the class of problems which you call co-adaptation. Here, as you say, Kilner helped the colonists ... and, as you have also said, perhaps such problems would not have been insuperable even without expert help. But I am a diplomat, and I find in these reports evidence of another set of problems altogether: the problems experienced by human beings extracted from one set of historical circumstances and introduced into another which is totally alien – and you'll appreciate, I'm sure, that I use the word "alien" here in a rather different sense. The question I must ask is this: Can men environmentally adapted to the kind of society we have today – or had a hundred or two hundred years ago – readapt themselves and their social precepts to the kind of circumstances which they find on the colony worlds? You talk about biological adaptation, Alex, but I am thinking more of social adaptation. It is possible that in the ancient world there were many human societies which could have provided colonists capable of surviving on an alien world ... the Cro-Magnons, the Kalahari bushmen, the pygmies of the Ituri forest ... these people possessed cultures adapted to the business of survival without technology, without material possessions. But such cultures no longer exist. There is no man on Earth who lives now in a society without wealth and without the produce of technology. In making these men into colonists, are we not trying to turn back the cultural clock? Is this practical ... and if not, how can we make it practical? Do you see what I mean?'

'I see,' said Alexander.

'In the future,' said Pietrasante, 'the whole philosophy of colonisation may have to change. We may have to think very seriously about training colonists in a much more extreme sense than the last project did. But first, we must look much more closely at the present colonies, and find out why they are as they are. We must redefine our concepts of possible and impossible, in this area. We must ask questions that have not been asked before.'

'It isn't my field,' said the biologist.

'Of course not,' said the UN man hastily. 'I'm not trying to redefine your job, at this late stage. The role which you have to play will be the same role that Kilner played ... except for one thing.'

'What you're trying to tell me is that I won't be in charge. You're demoting me.'

'It's not a matter of demotion, Alex. You will be in charge of your own side of the mission. But there will be another side. You must see how necessary it is. In view of Kilner's reports we simply can't restrict the scope of the *Daedalus* missions to biology ... to ratcatching, if you'll forgive the use of the vulgar term. You'll be the sole authority in your own field, and your status will remain the same. The only difference is that your lab staff will be cut to two. The man in charge of the sociological study will take over the diplomatic functions which Kilner handled so badly. His name is Nathan Parrick – he's a historian and a social anthropologist.'

'But if we're jointly in charge,' objected Alexander, 'who makes the ultimate decisions? Divided authority can lead to problems.'

'Authority would be divided in any case,' Pietrasante pointed out. 'In all matters pertaining to the conduct of the ship itself the captain is the final authority. You and Nathan will be engaged in tasks which are somewhat different in nature, but your interests should be very similar. There should be no difficulties in coming to an agreement over any question which concerns you both. If any deadlock does arise, Captain Rolving will arbitrate.'

Alexander stared out of the window for a moment or two, turning the matter over in his mind.

'Who are the staff I have left?' he asked finally.

'Conrad Silvian – he was with Kilner and his experience should be invaluable. We couldn't even consider leaving him out. The other berth went to Linda Beck. Did you meet her?'

Alexander nodded.

'I'm sure they'll be adequate to any task which you have to face.'

'I'm sure they will,' said the biologist. 'Qualitatively speaking. But why only two? If there are two crew members and Parrick, that leaves one berth unaccounted for, doesn't it? Or does Parrick have an assistant?'

'In a manner of speaking,' said Pietrasante. 'The seventh member of the expedition will, in fact, be under his authority. But she is not exactly an assistant. Her name is Mariel Valory. She's a talent.'

'What kind of talent?'

'It's what they call in common parlance "the gift of tongues". She is extraordinarily adept with languages. She is, of course, very young, and the idea of giving her a place on the expedition was opposed by some members of our team. I myself was doubtful of the wisdom of including her. But in view of the questions raised by Kilner's reports it seemed most important that we should provide the second expedition with better information-collecting facilities. We want to provide as broad a base to the areas of intellectual inquiry as possible. It is obvious that Kilner completely failed to open up any constructive areas of communication with the colonists which he contacted. He arrived to find them hostile, and despite the help he gave them he never overcame that hostility. We hope that Mariel will help to offset this difficulty.

'In addition, there is another compelling reason. You are scheduled to recontact six colonies. Two of these colonies were established on worlds where the reports of the survey teams suggested that there were already intelligent life-forms. Although these species had no discernible culture or civilisation, it was suggested that they had language and a certain degree of social organisation. The framework within which the survey teams operated did not permit further investigation of these lines of inquiry, but the colonists dispatched to these worlds were instructed to make all possible attempts to open channels of communication with these life-forms. On these two worlds, if nowhere else, Mariel's talent may prove to be of crucial importance.'

'How old is she?' asked Alexander.

'Fourteen. I *know* that it's very young, Alex, but she's advanced for her age in the intellectual sense. And fourteen is not only above the age of consent but above the age of majority in a great many countries. Talents burn out, Alex, and if we want to use them we have to use them young.'

After a pause, Alexander said, 'You're certainly hitting me with everything at once, aren't you? I've been in on this project for months, and this is the first I've heard of *any* of this. Oh, I know that I joined when plans were still in a very fluid state, and that my ideas don't count for much in the planning because I'm only the poor bastard that has to go out there, and not one of the UN execs with a career in politics to think about ... but, Nico, this is the eleventh hour! Only now do you show me Kilner's reports. Only now do you tell me my staff's been cut, that I'm now only joint leader of the expedition with your pet diplomat, and that there's a child on the strength as well. Do you think that's fair? Suppose I were to turn around now and tell you that if this is the way things are going to be you can count me out?'

'You won't do that,' said Pietrasante.

'No,' said the other. 'I won't. You know damn well I won't. But you're sure as hell trespassing on my good nature.'

'Nathan Parrick is a good man,' said the UN man. 'And he's not a pet diplomat. He *is* a diplomat ... but he's also a brilliant social scientist. You have a good deal in common. And a lot of the work he'll take off your shoulders is work you wouldn't want to be bothered with in any case. You're a scientist, not a politician. You don't want to get bogged down in petty disputes with the colonists, in negotiations and recriminations. You want to get on with your job. If only Kilner had been allowed to get on with his job instead of being involved in constant hassles with the people he was trying to help. ... This is all for the best, Alex. I'm sorry we couldn't tell you sooner, but you don't realise the amount of backstage argument that has gone into this. The UN is run by committees – the whole *world* is run by committees – and nothing ever gets done or decided until the eleventh hour. You know the way things are.'

'Oh sure,' said Alexander wearily. 'I know exactly how things are. It's a wonder the whole damn world doesn't grind to a halt.'

'It has,' said Pietrasante. 'That's part of the problem. Perhaps the most desperate part of all.'

Outside the car, night was gathering. Very slowly, darkness consumed the daylight. But the stars never came out, for the sky never lost the ruddy glow that was the reflection of the lights of sprawling civilisation. Over the cities, the air was always hazy. Only the moon occasionally shone through.

There were no horizons in the sky, but from the city streets there was no glimpse of infinity either.

CHAPTER ONE

The air in the hall was heavy with heat and odour. At first, it had been a welcome change from the cool, sterile air aboard the ship, but it didn't take long before I began to feel slightly sick. I wasn't acclimatised, and I hadn't drunk enough ... or maybe I'd drunk too much.

I kept looking for an opportunity to get outside and take time to recover, wondering whether they'd be offended. But Nathan Parrick was playing the star role – the ambassador from Earth – and the time came when I figured that they'd hardly miss the odd spear-carrier. Several heads turned to watch me go, but their glances were incurious and nobody tried to haul me back into the party with an excess of drunken zeal.

I don't like parties, anyhow.

The noise seemed somehow louder as it oozed out after me than it had been when I was in the middle of it. I suppose that was because I had the silence to compare it to. Outside, there was a light breeze and the sun was going down. There was not a soul in sight. To get away from the intrusive sound I went down the steps and began to walk away, into the village. I was, I suppose, walking down what one day might become the main street, but for the time being the conglomeration of buildings lacked that much organisation. The hall where the welcoming party was staggering on towards the evening hours was simply the geometrical centre of a loosely knit community extending on all sides. The distribution of homes and outhouses obeyed – in a rough and ready fashion – the inverse square law. Even the farm where the ship rested, which was something more than a mile to the west, was 'in' the village – a part of the community whose focal point this was.

I'd gone maybe twenty or thirty paces when I heard some-one coming after me. The feet fell lightly, and I knew with-out looking back that it wasn't one of the natives. I waited, but didn't turn until she was level with me. It was Karen Karelia, the spare ship-jockey.

'Fleeing in disgust?' she asked. The hint of irony was rarely missing from her voice. Peter Rolving, whose position as captain she affirmed by fulfilling the role of 'crew', de-scribed her as a space freak, implying that she wanted off Earth largely because she wasn't fond of her fellow men. She was crazy enough, of course – you have to be certifiable to want to ride a starship – but she wasn't really a volunteer alien.

'I just want to look around before it gets dark,' I told her. 'Why should I be disgusted?'

'Doesn't it strike you as being a little over-extravagant? The food . . . the people . . . the way they're working so hard to pretend that it's a momentous occasion?'

'It is,' I pointed out. 'First contact in five generations, maybe six. The first of the sardine cans must have landed nearly a hundred and eighty years ago, the last . . . well, maybe one-forty, give or take a few.'

'But it isn't quite what we expected, is it?' she said.

I looked around, at the neat buildings grouped about the hall. There was a store, which had been extended within the last few years so that it now looked like two buildings tacked together. Its business must still be expanding as more and more goods came in from outside. There was a black-smith's shop. There were three great barns, semicircular in section, which – at the proper season – might be filled with the produce of the whole village preparatory to its being loaded into wagons and hauled away.

'I didn't come with any fixed notions,' I told her. 'No, this isn't what Kilner found. Here, for once, the colony seems to have been successful. It looks good. And they weren't ready to cut our throats when we came out through the lock . . . on the contrary, they seemed delighted to see us, even if it did take Nathan half an hour to explain who and what we are.'

'But you sound as if you can't quite believe it,' she said,

'whether you expected the unexpected or not. And you've got to admit that they come as something of a surprise. Damn it all, half of them are getting on for seven feet tall!'

I began to walk on, and she walked with me. We headed for a small stone bridge over the stream which cut a curved path through the village.

'It's odd,' I agreed.

'What's caused it?'

'Maybe they eat well,' I said. It wasn't a sarcastic remark, but she took it as such.

'I know people back home who made eating the purpose of their lives,' she said. 'People who knew just about everything there is to know about stuffing themselves full of every goddamn edible thing under the sun. They grew fat, but they didn't grow seven feet tall.'

'We're under a different sun now,' I pointed out.

She allowed me to dismiss the question without beginning to take it seriously. Inside, though, it was the thing that worried me most. The people looked healthy, happy, and strong. Very strong. A race of giants. People do grow that big on Earth – occasionally. There are a handful of giants in every generation. It's natural ... there's nothing so very strange about it. But when *everybody* is built like an Olympic hammer-thrower ... you have to wonder whether you're not discovering a different order of nature altogether.

But there was time to think about such questions. Abundant time. For now, though, I was on an alien world for the first time. I was walking on alien soil, beneath a different sky. I was beset by a strange mixture of sensations – a combination of familiarity and strangeness. It was absurd that the sky should be blue, that the sun sinking towards the horizon should have just the same ruddy face, the distant clouds hazing its face should be the same clouds that floated over the Earth. Superficially, the familiarity concealed the alien. But there was the *knowledge*, inside me, that *everything* here was different. The sun and the sky were *not* the ones I knew, but were merely in disguise. The lack of any real sensory confirmation of the fact that this world was Floria, ninety light-years from Earth, and not the Earth itself, made

me feel that this was all an elaborate façade ... a sham ...
and feel that there was something weird and terrible lurking
just out of sight in the corner of my eye.

I stopped to lean on the parapet of the bridge, to look
down into the water of the stream. It was only a couple of
feet deep, but the rippled surface was so full of shadows and
the red reflected glow of the sun that I couldn't see anything
beneath it.

'No fish at all,' murmured Karen.

'None whatsoever,' I agreed. Here was a point of essential
difference. But it was a covert difference. Even if I had been
able to see the depths beneath the surface, how could my
senses have told me 'This is not Earth ... because there is no
fish to be seen'? There were no fish in the streams of Earth.
Only in the farms and the factories, where the water flowed
in sculpted channels, artificially aerated and ther-
mostatically adjusted.

She pulled herself up on to the parapet and used its
height as a vantage point from which to look out at the
village – but the stream itself was in a gully, and she could see
little more from here than from the steps of the hall whence
we had set out. I scanned the buildings incuriously, but my
powers of observation worked uncontrolled, and my brain
processed their information as a matter of habit.

I noted that the buildings – each and every one, whether
home or hut, brick or stone or wood, great or small – seemed
curiously *unfinished*. There was not a one that had been
architecturally planned. They had been put up quickly, each
to serve their function, with the assumption that each one
might be constantly rebuilt – improved and extended. Each
building had a life of its own. They were capable of growth
and change, perhaps even of metamorphosis.

It was a small thing, but it seemed meaningful. No one
built that way on Earth. Here, the community was in a constant state of remaking itself: reshaping and replanning and
reforming. They were unaffected by insidious myths of opti-
mum use of resources and ultimate ends. There was a re-
laxation in the way things were done here, and a tension in
the way they were done on Earth.

'Perhaps it's a local thing,' said Karen.

'What?'

'The giant business. Perhaps they're inbred, perhaps it's a freak.'

'I don't think so,' I said.

She was sitting on the parapet now, with her legs dangling down towards the water.

'What happens tomorrow?' she asked.

'They've sent a messenger to the nearest town. It's on the coast. Nathan and I will go there in the morning, try to arrange meetings with the various people in authority. I don't know whether it will be initially necessary for Mohammed to go to the mountain or whether they'll come to us. Local transport isn't very fast, although I hear they have the beginnings of a railroad. It may take a while to make the necessary contacts, but once we have channels of communications open it will get easier. What we need is a house – or a couple of houses – in the village, and people to handle liaison. Nathan and I may have to do a fair amount of travelling in the first few months, though.'

'You think we'll stay the full year? Even if things are really as healthy and happy as they seem?'

'Almost certainly. If the colony is a success and doesn't need our help, all well and good ... but we'll want to know *why* it's a great success just as much as we'd want to know why it was in trouble. There's a lot of work to be done. The whole question of whether there's to be a new colony programme may depend on the information we bring back – and from that point of view analysing and documenting the successes may be even more vital than analysing and documenting the failures.'

'*If* it really is a success,' she said.

'If ...' I echoed noncommittally.

'You say they have a railroad,' she said. 'Steam engines, I presume. ... Is that good or bad, after all this time? What sort of technological level are they supposed to have reached?'

I shrugged. 'Silly question,' I said, in an offhand manner. 'There are no "levels of technology". Such things are an artifact of history. Maybe the notion has some meaning when you consider the order in which new discoveries are likely to be made – but there's no coherent chain effect like a row of dominoes falling over. Here, where the colonists started out with all the knowledge of science and technology Earth could provide them with, and were limited only by the speed at which they could begin to muster the physical resources, technological developments would crop up in an entirely different order.'

'But there are no tractors in the fields and horses do most of the work. They obviously don't have internal combustion engines. Why not?'

'Maybe they haven't struck oil,' I suggested. 'Or maybe they decided to do without. One advantage of having all that knowledge at your fingertips is that you can also decide which inventions you *don't* want. Hindsight may have suggested to the old leaders of the colony that petrol engines are one thing the New Arcadia can do without. I don't know ... but did you see those magnificent horses? It isn't just the people here that grow big and strong. There might be a lot to be said for a simpler way of life. Look where five centuries of industrial revolution got us on Earth.'

'And you reckon that's OK? The colony lands, burns the books, and starts over from scratch?'

'That's not what I said,' I pointed out. 'They keep the books, and they use them. Only they aren't simple-minded about it. They don't just look to the books to tell them what to do – they look into them and try to figure out what *not* to do as well. The colonists were taking big risks to leave Earth ... they must really have hated it. So why would they want to set out and slavishly recreate it? No ... if this colony *is* succeeding, the men behind it will have had something up their sleeve ... something that had *allowed* it to succeed.'

'You really want to find something like that, don't you?' she said. 'A magic formula. Something to save the entire colony concept, renew the whole effort.'

I studied her carefully. She had a hard, bony face, framed by white-blonde hair which grew wild all around it. She was thirty-some, and didn't look as if she'd done a lot of smiling in her life. Her sense of humour was decidedly acid. I liked her.

'OK,' I said. 'So I would. If there were such a thing to be found. But I'm not an idiotic optimist. I believe in the colony project even if there *is* no magic formula. I think we should keep trying, in spite of setbacks. I think we've done what we can with Earth. We have to move on to new levels of ambition.'

I almost expected her to sneer, but she didn't. 'A lot of people think that kind of talk is poison,' she commented.

'Not out here,' I said.

'Don't bet on it.'

'What do you mean?'

'What I said,' she muttered tersely.

She couldn't be talking about the colonists – she had to be thinking evil thoughts about someone on the strength. So who was on board to play devil's advocate? Nathan? She wasn't going to say. Maybe she was talking about herself. Maybe she meant to imply nothing more than the fact that other people didn't quite have my deep-seated conviction about the rightness of it all.

'It'll be dark pretty soon,' she said, changing the subject.

The sun was squatting on the horizon, but twilight might last some time. She wasn't trying to pick an argument, though . . . just putting things back together again.

'No point in taking a long walk,' I said. 'They haven't got street lights yet. Maybe they're waiting till they have streets.'

'It wouldn't be very romantic anyhow,' she said, with the irony back at full force. 'Not without a moon.'

'That's one hell of an old joke,' I said. 'And it wasn't ever funny.'

'Don't take it to heart,' she said.

I suddenly felt slightly embarrassed, as though the sarcasm were directed specifically at me, instead of just coming naturally. I moved away reflexively, and then turned the movement into a first strolling step back in the direction of the hall.

'Maybe they're missing us,' I said. 'It might be your turn to make a speech.'

'Sure,' she countered. 'I'd be a big hit. Every single dirty joke that's been made up back home in the last two hundred years will be new to these guys.'

'Don't bet on it,' I told her.

CHAPTER TWO

There was a lot of the evening still to be endured. I say 'endured' because it really wasn't my scene at all. I'm not antisocial, but I find humanity en masse something of an embarrassment of riches. I don't like crowds. Few scientists do. Once you have given over your life to the study of abstract principles governing the behaviour of things which have only to be observed, never communicated with, your attitude to your fellow humans begins to change, and keeps on changing. A gap opens up between you, and no matter how close you stand to other people there's an intangible distance forbidding a complete meeting of the minds. The distancing effect is even worse, of course, when the fellow human in question is one with whom you have nothing in common ... not even a cultural background. In such instances, it is far too easy for said fellow human to become another thing to be observed, to be placed in a context of abstract and generalised principles rather than a context of social interaction.

I have to confess that I could only watch the Florians from within. I could not reach out and join them. I could not enjoy the social occasion that they had concocted for our benefit, despite the fact that they were friendly. I didn't, as Karen had suggested, find them disgusting ... but there is something intimidating about men who tower over you by a

32

full foot when, throughout your life, you have thought of yourself as a tall man.

Nathan Parrick, however, seemed to be in his element. It wasn't difficult to imagine his life on Earth consisting of endless official functions and informal but incredibly important meetings with all manner of VIPs. He walked easily and quickly, with the happy gift of being able to say nothing at all in the nicest possible way.

There *were* speeches. Nathan's was excellent, though lacking in dirty jokes. The ones which the farmers' self-elected leader, Vern Harwin, attempted to deliver were by no means excellent but had a certain ring of sincerity which I found rather comforting. He didn't tell any dirty jokes either.

They were showing off, of course. (And so were we, in return.) The food and drink which they'd provided was too abundant, and so was the spirit of fellowship. Everybody laughed too loudly, said all the things they thought they ought to say. Everyone felt the need to make an impression.

The farmers didn't know that other colonies had failed, were in the process of failing. They didn't know that they were, from our point of view, a great surprise. But they did know – or, at least, they believed – that they were, in their own right, a colossal successs. They were proud of themselves and of their world. They *loved* showing off.

And they felt, somehow, superior to us. They couldn't conceal it. We were smooth-talking visitors from the parental world (which to them could only be an awesome myth), had arrived in our great black skyborne cylinder, representatives of a 'higher' civilisation. And yet they felt superior. Because they were bigger? Or because the memory of Earth that survived within their culture was a memory of a failed world . . . a world which had lost its way in a history controlled by fortune?

These people were cocksure. They had a wealth of pride. And that made me uneasy . . . for in every land of milk and honey lurks a rat, and the difference between proud people and humble ones is that the humble ones are aware of the rat *before* it starts picking their bones.

But they were only farmers. I told myself that. Somewhere in this world would be shrewder men. They would be afraid of us – perhaps they might hate us – but they would be able to tell us what we wanted to know.

Five of us had come to the party. Standing orders required two people to stay with the ship at all times. Rolving had insisted on being one, and somehow it had been agreed that Linda Beck should be the other. After two weeks in transit, no doubt we could all have used a sight of the sky and a breath of air, but a fortnight isn't an eternity, by any means – which meant, among other things, that the relief at being free from the confining walls of the ship wore off fairly quickly. As the party dragged on, I watched the others wilt, and began to count the minutes. Only Nathan maintained his front of inexhaustibility.

Conrad seemed to be maintaining himself aloof from it all. He'd drunk a fair amount but he was cold sober. He had a head like concrete – nothing ever threatened his presence of mind. He was fifty, but looked older. He was tall, by Earthly standards, but life was beginning to drain his flesh and he no longer looked strong. His hair was white, and there was something birdlike about him: perhaps the suggestion of the way he held his head to expose his neck, or his uncommonly bright eyes.

He alone, of the team who had gone out with Kilner, had elected to go out again. A five-year turn of duty followed quickly by seven: a punishing sequence. Perhaps he had expected to take Kilner's place, although I had never detected the slightest sign of resentment in his attitude towards me.

The noise seemed simply to roll around Conrad like the ocean waves around a rock. He was unmoved by it. Karen and I endured it. Mariel, though, seemed at once to be absorbed within it and pained by it. Mariel was fourteen. I couldn't help thinking of fourteen as being very young. . . . I had, after, all, a son some three years older. She seemed to me to have no place aboard the ship, no place in such a venture as ours. And she made me uneasy. I knew, although I had not yet seen any outward evidence of the fact, that her mind was not like mine. She seemed to me far more alien than these men of Floria – or the truly alien creatures of Floria. They fit. She did not. One expects strangers in strange lands. But not within the sanctified enclave of home.

I found myself watching her as she reacted and replied to the questions flung at her from all sides. The Florians understood her presence no more than I did. To them, she must seem even younger, for although she had not yet grown into her frame she would never be tall ... not even by Earthly standards. She seemed neither lively nor particularly interested in what was going on, and yet the colonists – particularly the women – seemed to feel it necessary to keep her constantly involved. Their questions were inane ... though they genuinely wanted to know about Earth they could not find the right questions to ask. Not of Mariel ... not even of Nathan.

I think we were all profoundly glad when the affair broke up. They asked us politely if we wished to stay in the village, though finding five beds for us would undoubtedly have proved difficult. When we expressed a preference for our bunks in the ship they offered us lanterns to light our way through the dark night. The farmer whose house was close to the ship, and whose field we had destroyed by landing on it, adopted the role of guide. His name was Joe Saccone.

We took our time walking back, and made no effort to stay in a close-knit group. I dropped back deliberately, in order to talk to Conrad Silvian. He had charge of one of the lanterns, and thus it didn't matter how far behind we fell.

'What do you think?' I asked him.

'About things in general? Or the size of things in particular?'

'Both.'

'In general,' he said, his voice dry and slow, 'things are good. Better than I saw on the first trip. This community is well established and working. They talk of towns and cities, and they have only a vague notion of the things which are going on in the far west – in the forests and the mountains. The colony is big, complex ... and *relaxed*. We found nothing like this on the first trip. The colonists on those worlds knew exactly what was going on everywhere, because

35

the whole operation was tightly knit, geared to survival. They'd never got beyond the point where any group of men could survive independent of the efforts of the whole colony. Here we have a kind of cultural diffusion – the parts becoming independent of the whole. I think that's promising ...'

'But ...' I supplied.

'But,' he agreed, 'something is happening here and it's strange. The wrong way around. We came expecting to find deficiency disease, and what we find is *superficiency* disease. People on Earth grow to be seven feet tall and stay fit and healthy. They may make damn good sportsmen. They tend to die twenty years ahead of their three score and ten even without taking environmental effects into account, but there's an awful lot of small men would trade years for size. So maybe this is a good sign, too. Maybe these are a better breed of men, growing big and strong in their alien Eden. *They* think so. But I want to know why. Rigorous natural selection for height and mass is out of the question – any subtractive selection strong enough to add a foot and more to the average height in seven generations would have decimated the colony. So ... it seems that something is affecting their glandular balance, altering the control of growth. There are steroid drugs on Earth which permit the body to put on a lot of weight by acting as hormone mimics and upsetting the metabolic balance. They don't usually add height, but they're not usually given to growing children. If something in the alien plants that have been conscripted as food fit for humans has such an effect, it would be perpetually present, and might permanently affect the hormonal balance.'

'That's possible,' I agreed.

'We'll be able to find out in the lab,' he said. 'But it would help us to look if we could find out about their eating habits.'

'It might also be worth asking a few simple questions about the population size, birth rates, death statistics, and so on,' I mused. 'And we mustn't overlook the possibility that this may be a local condition. We're looking at one tight-knit group. Maybe in the towns – or in similar communities a

36

long way away — there's a wider range of heights. Maybe somewhere atavisms like us still survive. You know ... pygmies.'

He didn't laugh. It wasn't funny. Anything you can't understand is something to worry about ... especially the simple things. Sometimes you can leap to the obvious conclusion and be hopelessly wrong. The history of science is the history of people belatedly realising the obvious and still being wrong.

We lagged so far behind the others that by the time we got back to the ship there was no queue for the safety lock. The lock took two at a time, and we were able to go through together. Another advantage in being slow was that the burden of answering what's-it-like? questions posed by Linda and Pete Rolving fell principally on other shoulders. Even so, we didn't entirely get away with it, because Linda wanted specialist impressions as well as general ones, and Conrad and I were the natural ones to provide them. Between us, we went over most of the ground we'd covered in our earlier conversation.

I finally got to my bunk feeling utterly weary, but with my mind still in a high gear. I lay back on the sleeping-bag, trying to slow things down inside my head. I was just about easing back when there was a knock at the door. It was Mariel. I'm afraid that my tone as I asked her what she wanted was mildly hostile.

'I thought you ought to know,' she said. 'Those people in the village. They really meant it.'

'What do you mean?' I asked.

'They're honest people. They aren't hostile. They put on a show — but it wasn't really false.'

I hadn't got up from the bunk. I let my head rest on the pillow while I stared at her for a few moments.

'You mean that you can tell when people are lying?' I said finally.

'Usually,' she replied.

'And they weren't. They really were pleased to see us. They really think that everything here is going well. Unlike the people in Kilner's colonies.'

'That's right.'

'Why tell me? I'm just the ratcatcher. Nathan's the contact man.'

'You seemed worried . . . as if you weren't sure of them.'

'And you thought you'd take the weight off my mind?'

'Yes.' I could see that the bluntness of my comments was wounding her. She was holding the door ajar, and her fingers were moving slightly as she gripped it. I felt contrite, but I couldn't disguise the uneasiness which was constricting my voice. I hadn't known that her talent extended to being a lie detector. I didn't really know how far her talent extended at all, or what it consisted of. The vague notion that she might, to some extent, be able to read the thoughts behind my words was disturbing.

'I'm sorry,' I said, a little more kindly. 'Thanks for telling me.'

'Do you know why they're so big?' she asked hesitantly.

'No,' I replied, wondering whether she was asking because she didn't know or because she did.

'Neither do they,' she told me. 'They didn't realise . . . it's normal with them . . . they didn't know that they were different from the original colonists. . . .' She searched for more words, but failed to find them. She had the gift of tongues . . . but it was the gift of understanding, not of speaking.

'Didn't they, now?' I said, sitting up, and feeling my mind get back into gear. I looked at her carefully. She had nothing more to say of her own accord, and was waiting rather anxiously for questions. She pulled the door open a little further, ready to go.

'How can you tell when people are lying?' I asked gently.

She shrugged slightly. 'Reflexes,' she said. 'Most people can't control the little physical signs which go with their thoughts. Your pupils dilate when you look at people you like, the muscles in your face change when you react inside your head to things which happen. I . . . just decode the signals. I don't know how . . . it's not really conscious. But I've been tested. That's how I do it. I have to see people, close to . . . I can't read minds.'

I wondered what she could read from my face. I knew she knew I was wondering. Even if she couldn't get inside my head, there was still cause for uneasiness. Who can tell when his pupils are dilating?

'If they don't realise it's happened,' I reasoned, aloud, 'then it must have happened over several generations, and uniformly throughout the population.' I looked at her for confirmation. She said nothing, and if there were signs in her face, I couldn't read them. But then logic wasn't her department. What she wanted was some acknowledgment of the fact that she'd been right to tell me – and some apology for the fact that I hadn't been ready to listen.

'You're right,' I said. 'It is important. Next time, I'll ... well, I just didn't realise. Thanks.'

Without so much as a smile, she disappeared. I looked back at the words, and tried to sort out what thoughts had mingled with them as I'd spoken. I knew what I'd said ... but what had I said *to her*?

I lay back again, and for the second time I tried to unwind.

But I couldn't get to sleep. I turned over and over and over, knowing that I was tired, but my thoughts just wouldn't die away. They clouded over, but they remained loud, and made themselves heard. Trying to exclude sensory impressions merely left my mind awash with ideas, memories, half-formed sentences. My attention leaped from point to point in bizarre sequences controlled by the imagistic logic of the mind, often devoid of all apparent reason.

Hours passed before consciousness slowly and reluctantly yielded its grip upon me.

CHAPTER THREE

I was glad to get up when the morning came. I felt as if I'd had no sleep at all, but such impressions are usually false. I'd lost track of time, and that in itself is a kind of rest from the measured regime of consciousness.

I found most of the others already up and about, discussing how they might best make use of the day or two we had in hand before contact was made with the appropriate authority. Only Nathan and I were committed to the trip into town, and it seemed wisest for the rest to stay close to the ship. For the moment, five of us went to the nearby house. The farmer had offered us breakfast, and it was there that Vern Harwin would meet us with transport to take us into town. The two who stayed within the ship were Pete and Conrad.

The atmosphere prevailing in the house bore no resemblance whatsoever to the hall of the night before. It was quiet, and unhurried, and the silence was perhaps a little embarrassed. Conversation did not flourish. Joe Saccone was by no means the extrovert that Harwin was, and his wife hardly paused long enough to exchange more than half a dozen words at a time. They had children, but we didn't see them. They were, it seemed, already out working. I wasn't quite sure why they'd been banished . . . for the sake of convenience, or because the farmer wanted to keep them away from us.

The main room of the house, where the family lived and ate, was clean and tidy. It also seemed to me to be *empty*: empty not merely of things, but also of personality. There was none of the kind of superfluous trivia which tends to accumulate wherever people make their homes. The aspect of the room and all its contents was essentially functional. I cast my mind back into my hazy knowledge of history, trying to imagine what kind of world the original colonists had left, what kind of assumptions and prejudices they might have carried with them to the stars and embedded in the structure of their new society.

It had been a time of crisis, of course – the resource crisis and the economic crisis and the population crisis had been perpetual even then. What made the difference between that time and the present was not the crisis but the manner of the reaction to it. Those had been days of violent rejection of old assumptions, demands for action. It had been a hot-tempered period. It had been dominated by the ethic of *make for use* ... the criminality of waste, the condemnation of luxury. There had been anti-art movements in America and Europe, when a great deal of what had formerly been treasured as 'artistic heritage' had been destroyed. There were the media riots, campaigns to destroy private transport. ...

It all seemed very vague and faraway. But there were, it seemed to me, echoes of the zeitgeist here, on this world. The people here had not recovered a mania for acquisition, although circumstances might permit such a thing. They still made for *use*. They still seemed to waste very little – not materials, not effort. But, as time progressed, could they possibly maintain such an ethic? Someone once commented that those who fail to respect history are condemned to repeat it. Would that happen here? Or did these people have something left to them by the original colonists that would not die, and which might help them into a new direction of social evolution?

Breakfast consisted of bread and soup. It was a vegetarian meal, for a variety of reasons. Floria had only extremely limited animal life – only simple invertebrates had evolved here. That meant that pigs and horses had had to be imported along with the colonists – an unusual step for the old Colony Commission to have taken. Pigs and horses are heavy. There's a world of difference between shipping a couple of thousand eggs across ninety light-years to give a new world the basis of a chicken population and shipping large mammals. It had had to be done, however. People need meat and work-animals. The relationship between the colonists and their imported animals had, however, been a strange one. On an alien world, there was a kinship between man and horse, and between man and pig, that simply did not exist on Earth. It seemed that as a consequence of this the colonists did not eat horseflesh at all, and had gathered about the business of slaying and eating pigs a kind of ritual – a system of taboos. We had eaten pork at the welcoming party, but that had been a public occasion and a ceremonious one. Breakfast was bread and vegetable soup.

The bread was made from imported corn. The soup contained, I think, a mixture of vegetables brought from Earth and some of the native plants adopted by the colonists. It tasted rich and rather sweet.

The organic correspondence factor evaluating the degree of biochemical similarity between Floria's life-system and Earth's was eighty-eight: just about the highest the survey teams had ever found. There ought to be plenty of native plants perfectly edible and worth cultivating. I was tempted to go into the question with Joe, but there just wasn't time. Harwin turned up before we'd finished . . . not that any of us actually did finish, because the meal was scaled to Florian standards.

Nathan and I left the others to continue the business of nurturing friendly interplanetary relations at the grass-roots level, and mounted Vern Harwin's cart. There was room for three to sit up front, which was perhaps as well considering the strong agricultural smell emanating from the back.

'How long will it take to get to the town?' asked Nathan of Harwin.

'Not long,' was the reply. Harwin had no watch. There probably weren't more than a handful of clocks in the village. Nathan didn't pursue the point.

'Did the messenger who went to tell them we were coming get back yet?' I asked.

Harwin nodded.

'Did he say anything?'

Harwin shrugged. 'The people in South Bay will handle things. They didn't send any messages back.'

I gave up. Apparently, we had to wait and see. Harwin seemed to have only vague notions about things which did not actually involve him. It wasn't really surprising, but it was a little frustrating. There was no point in trying to find out most of the things we wanted to know here.

We passed through the village and moved into open countryside again. Cultivated fields stretched in all directions, and small clusters of buildings were dotted randomly over the whole area. It seemed very Earth-like, but we were in a region which had at one time been cleared of all native vegetation so that imported crops could be sown. To some extent the Earth crops had now been replaced by Florian ones, but the techniques of artificial cultivation had made sure that the alien plants did not seem too strange. All the vegetation was exceptionally rich – the Earth plants as well as the native ones flourished in this soil and grew well. There was little enough contrast because the Florian plants were green, and the range of shades was not dissimilar to the range of their counterparts. The actual photosynthetic agent was not chlorophyll, but it was designed to the same operational specifications and with the same optimal characteristics. This is not always the case on worlds which may be classified as Earth-like in purely physical terms, but unless the empirical chemical foundation of a planetary life-system are fairly similar to those of Earth's life-system colonisation is not possible. On all worlds to be successfully used by man, the building blocks of life have to be the same. The proteins and complex carbohydrates are always liable to be different, but the simple amino acids and hexose sugars which form their structural units are almost invariably the same. The limits of chemical possibility are ultimately binding and not all that wide (given identical physical conditions). There are only so many ways that you can build a molecule out of a handful of carbon, hydrogen, and oxygen atoms. Natural selection operates between chemicals as well as between organisms, and the ones recruited to do various specific jobs are generally very similar. Hence, Floria's chlorophyll-substitute looked and acted like chlorophyll.

But what holds true for chemical evolution does not hold true for the evolution of organisms. It isn't until you first set foot on alien soil that you begin to realise how large a role

43

pure chance has played in the design of Earth's biosphere. This applies far more to animals than plants, but even the Florian plants – to my trained eyes, at least – showed their alienness in their structure.

The casual observer screens out the unfamiliar and sees the familiar. A casual observer looking at the fields of alien crops planted by the colonists would see nothing odd. He would see leafy plants and grasses, huge bulbous fruits and seed-pods. But the casual observer has no real appreciation of complexity or of the various kinds of unity underlying complexity. The trained eye, however, screens out similarities and searches for the unfamiliar – not merely in the complexity of forms but in the kinds of unity underlying the complexity. The more my eyes searched the fields which we passed by in the cart as the two dray horses made their leisurely way along the rutted track, the more I was able to perceive the oddities which I had, until now, known only as remarks in reports written more than a century before.

Perhaps the most striking thing of all was the strict adherence to geometric principles practised by Floria's plants. Stems grew straight, foliage was arranged in an orderly fashion. Leaves tended to be precisely shaped, although the shapes were often very complex and three-dimensional – the curving of the photosynthetic sheets was as important and as precisely defined as the dimensions of the sheets themselves.

There were no pretty flowers because there were no insects to recruit to the business of pollination. However, though there were no birds and mammals either, there were fruits. Because most of the mobile life-forms on the world were saprophytes, preferring dead flesh to living, the fruits were grown only to rot. The seeds were usually tiny, and were picked up accidentally by the worms and the slugs which fed on the rotting fruit, either internally or externally, and were thus redistributed. The colonists, by taking the fruit early to eat while still fresh, were introducing a new factor into the whole balance of nature here.

Soon, we passed beyond the cultivated fields into the wilder land, where the Florian life-system still reigned supreme. There was no sign of invasion of this untouched land by

Earthly 'weeds'. The imported plants could not compete with the native ones on equal terms. Here, trees grew, and wild grasses in great profusion. There was not, however, the same degree of randomness as is seen in wild land on Earth. The geometrical compulsion was still clear, in the distribution of the plants as well as their forms. The trees grew tall, and they bent in the wind to show off a considerable degree of elasticity. Their branching was precise and ordered. They carried passengers: not merely parasites such as often infest the bodies of Earthly trees, but commensals using the structure without, apparently, inconveniencing the trees overmuch. The grasses were wide bladed and rather rigid, looking rather like clusters of crystals.

The Florian plants were photosynthetically more efficient than the Earth plants, not because of their chemical organisation but because of their structural design. An acre of Florian plants could fix a good deal more solar energy than an acre of plant cover in a comparable environment on Earth. This was, in a very literal sense, a land of plenty, where everything grew big and healthy. With nearly twice as much energy pouring *into* the biosphere, there was much more available at the top of every food chain. But there was also a very fast energy *turnover* here. The plants grew fast, but they also died quickly. The flesh-structures built with such calm efficiency decayed very quickly. That was why there was so much scope here for saprophytes ... so much scope that herbivores had never evolved. And just as herbivores had never evolved, neither had carnivores.

'Do you have much trouble keeping the native plants out of your fields?' I asked Harwin. 'It seems to me you might have difficulties with alien weeds.'

'They come back,' said the farmer laconically. 'But it's not too bad. We clear 'em out before planting. Some of them are real bastards — can grow a mile of root in a week, it seems. But we manage.'

'I suppose it's easier with the native crops, though,' I said.

'We don't get much trouble there,' he agreed.

'And a higher yield per acre?' I asked.

He nodded. 'In that case,' I said, 'one might expect that

all you farmers would be gradually switching over to native produce. The demand for it must have been low to start with, but over the years you must be slowly replacing the Earth stock with native plants.'

He turned to look at me then, and recognised with the slight nod that he gave me that I knew what I was talking about. I was right, and he was slightly surprised that I knew.

'It could be dangerous,' I commented, 'phasing out the Earth crops altogether.'

'Won't happen,' he said. 'Still a lot of prejudice. Lot of people in the towns won't eat nothing but the stuff that came with the ships. Out here . . . well, we grow the stuff. It comes out of the same soil, and we do the same work putting it in and taking it out. The difference don't seem so important to us, I suppose.'

Here, at last, was something useful. There were people who ate only traditional food . . . and yet they were presumably as big as the farmers who lived on a mixed diet . . . they had to be. Otherwise the correlation would have been too easy to miss. So it wasn't as simple as it seemed. It wasn't just something in the native food that made them grow.

'Does anyone live exclusively on native crops?' I asked.

'I don't know,' he said. 'Pigs, I guess. Don't see why not, but don't know that it ever happens, either. But like I said, out here we don't think so much of the difference. We just grow what we can, and what the people in town want. What's it matter which ones came with the first colonists and which were here when we arrived?'

And from his point of view, of course, it *didn't* much matter. So far as he was concerned, Floria was the one and only world, not one of a series of alien planets. To him, it was *all* familiar. And familiarity breeds . . . well, not always contempt, but at least contentment. It would be easy for these farmers to take too much for granted. Nothing in the alien life-system had ever proved inimical to human life . . . yet.

'There's someone coming,' said Nathan.

He had been listening to our conversation without manifesting any real interest, but now he was alert again. I shielded my eyes from the bright morning sun and looked ahead along the dirt road. About a mile away there was another horse-drawn vehicle approaching us. There was also a man on horseback. I thought, for a moment, that I saw several more horsemen some way off to the north, but when I tried to find them again with my eye they were out of sight. They were obviously not on the same road, in any case.

As we came closer, I saw that the other vehicle was a closed carriage. It looked like a miniature version of one of the ancient stage coaches used in the days of the American pioneers.

'Someone coming to meet us?' suggested Nathan.

'Must be,' muttered Harwin, with obvious displeasure. He had not anticipated our being taken out of his hands so soon, and he obviously felt that there was a certain amount of prestige to be gained as the man who arrived in South Bay with the visitors from Earth. There was, however, nothing he could do. I wondered why the messenger had not been told that someone would come out to collect us.

Several minutes passed before we eventually met and both vehicles came to a halt, the horses face to face and apparently thoroughly bored. The man on horseback stayed behind the carriage, whose driver simply stared into space. It was the man who descended from the vehicle who was in command.

He was as massive and powerful as Harwin, but the manner of his clothing left no doubt that he was a townsman. The cloth was less coarse, and the way he wore the garments made it clear that they were not merely functional, but had style – far more style, in fact, than our own clothes, which were simple plastic all-purpose garments. As Nathan stepped down to greet the newcomer it seemed that the big man was the representative of civilisation greeting a less-favoured cousin. They exchanged formal pleasantries while I climbed down, and Nathan introduced me to him.

His name was Arne Jason. He did not mention any official rank or title but was so obviously accustomed to authority that the omission seemed natural. He thanked Harwin for taking care of us, and we thanked him too. Harwin accepted all the thanks with something less than perfect grace, but with a philosophical attitude. At least the ship was near his village, and would remain the centre of affairs.

Nathan relaxed visibly as we transferred ourselves to the carriage. It was shaded from the sun, had upholstered seats, and smelled of polish ... altogether more to his taste than a farm cart. In addition, Jason was a man to whom he could talk. Nathan Parrick was the kind of person who grows visibly brighter in the company of people with whom he has something in common.

As the carriage turned around, Jason looked out of the window. He was wearing a smile which struck me as being somehow unpleasant. His face was not handsome, but it was impressive. The features were cleancut and the eyes were keen. There is an unreasoning prejudice which leads people to think that size and intelligence are inversely proportional, but this giant was obviously an intelligent man.

'I'm tempted to say,' he said smoothly. 'that it's been a long time, but why pretend to be the voice of history? This is ... completely unexpected. We had come to believe that Earth was finished with us. We have been working with that assumption.'

'Earth has passed through a kind of historical twilight zone,' explained Nathan. 'It has proved impossible to send out ships for nearly a hundred years. We should not have left it so long before recontacting you, but circumstances were against us.'

I studied Jason, half expecting him to say something along the lines of 'better late than never.' But he just smiled. I got the impression that he might have preferred never.

'I suppose,' said Nathan carefully, 'that the news of our arrival has caused a certain amount of confusion. We did try to contact you while we were still in space, but it appears that you have no radio equipment.'

Again, Jason made no reply to the comment. Instead, he said, 'I had not thought that we would be so very different. Have we changed so much in becoming Florians?'

I exchanged a quick glance with Nathan.

'It appears,' I said, 'that there have been changes. You

seem to have added twelve inches and sixty or seventy pounds to the average height and weight of the population here.'

'Floria,' he said, still smiling, 'is a good world. We have done well here. Is that what you came to find out?'

'We are recontacting all the colonies,' said Nathan. 'Restoring communication to the network of human cultures spread across the arm of the galaxy. There has been an unfortunate hiatus, but we have better ships now, and the resources to equip them properly. Primarily, we have come to offer you help – if you need any.'

I disapproved slightly of the misleading nature of the statement, although the only point at which the truth was really stretched was the use of the word 'ships' in the plural. But I kept quiet. It wasn't my scene.

'As simple as that?' said Jason.

'It's not that simple,' said Nathan. 'Our basic intention is to reopen communication and provide such help as we can ... but that can be quite a complicated business. We come to your world, you see, in complete ignorance. We know nothing about you. We have a great deal to learn, before we can establish any meaningful links. We don't know, for instance, what kind of government you have. You are taking us, I presume, to someone who can speak for the colony as a whole?'

'No one man can do that,' said Jason.

'That's what I mean,' said Nathan. 'It can be difficult opening meaningful channels of communication.'

'And can you speak for Earth?' asked Jason smoothly. 'The whole Earth?'

Nathan smiled apologetically. 'Not really,' he said. 'But in a purely practical sense, we represent Earth. Primarily, we represent Earth science. Our ship is a laboratory ... we are equipped to analyse and perhaps help you combat any problems you have encountered in adapting to your new world.'

Jason shook his head. 'We have no problems,' he said flatly. Maybe they had a proverb here; Beware of Earthmen bearing gifts. Nathan tried a different tack.

'I understand that the seat of government is several hundred miles away,' he said. 'I presume we will be able to reach it by rail.' He was fishing desperately for some information. Jason wasn't exactly forthcoming. I thought, personally, that a straightforward 'Where are we going?' might have served the purpose better.

'We'll have to take the train from South Bay,' agreed Jason. 'It won't take too long. Our ultimate destination won't be the capital, even though the administration of the colony is centred there. I'll take you to the Library. The Planners operate from there.'

'The Planners?'

'They're the men who guide the colony. They're the people you will want to talk to.'

My mind went back to what I'd said to Karen about the possibility of guiding history by the selective introduction of technology. No prizes for guessing, though – it was logical enough, in the circumstances.

'We can't move the ship, I'm afraid,' said Nathan. 'We set it down as close as possible to the location which was planned as a landing site for the first colony ship, but there's always an error factor – a few hundred miles isn't a great deal in terms of continental dimensions. The ship will have to serve as our operational base.'

'What operations are you intending to carry out?' asked Jason.

'Investigations into the co-adaptation process,' I interrupted.

'But we have no problems,' said Jason. 'As I have already told you.'

'If that's so,' I replied, 'I'm glad. But we'd like to know *why* you haven't.'

Nathan gave me a dirty look. I realised why as the giant pounced on the implication.

'You mean that other colonies *do* have such problems?' he asked. 'Serious ones?'

'Yes,' I said. I saw no point in denying it.

'Perhaps, then we have been lucky.'

'Perhaps,' I agreed.

There was a brief pause. Then Jason said, 'I'm sure that the location of the ship will pose no real problems. I'm sure the planners will be able to work with you wherever your base is. I'm sure that there will be a fruitful exchange of ideas. How long do you intend to be here?'

'We can't say, exactly,' said Nathan. 'A year, perhaps.'

'That's a long time.'

'We've been such a long time getting here. There's a lot to catch up on. But if you need no actual help, then we may not stay so long.'

'And what happens next?' asked the big man. 'Once you have forged your new links of communication, that is. What are your . . . long-range objectives?'

His tone was light and friendly. The inquiry was polite. But I didn't need Mariel's gift to guess what lay behind it. Jason didn't believe us. He didn't think that we'd come here to find out what Earth could do for Floria, but to find out what Floria could do for Earth. He was suspicious. And why not? A century and more had passed since the last shipment of colonists. We had shown no interest at all in the colony until now – until, it must seem from their point of view, they were beginning to win their struggle with the alien environment. They had conquered the world, in a metaphorical sense, and now here were men from Earth, landing in their fields, asking how they were getting along. They didn't hate us for leaving them alone so long, as the colonists on Kilner's recontact mission had, but they had no cause to treat this as some kind of joyous family reunion. The farmers had given us a good welcome, but to the Planners who were busy mapping out the future of this world our arrival – and the possibility of our interference – might be bad news indeed.

'We have no fixed long-term plans,' said Nathan. 'What happens in the future depends very much on what we find in the present. Until the recontact has been completed, the UN can hardly form a policy. The important thing, though, is to reopen communication. Once we can talk to one another, we can begin to talk about uniting the whole network of human worlds into some kind of interplanetary community.

51

There is only one human race, even though some of its fragments are widely scattered.'

'And some of them,' added Jason, 'have changed.'

The mention of change reminded me that there was still a question to be answered here. I had made little or no progress in figuring out why the Florians were giants. Perhaps it was time to get some answers.

'What's the size of your total population?' I asked him. 'How many people are there in the colony?'

His face changed. The smile disappeared, and for the first time his suspicions were clear in his expression. I realised that I had hit a nerve. I had asked the question in one context, but he had understood it in another. I wondered why it seemed to him to be such a nasty question. Was there some mystery here? Was there something he wanted to conceal?

'I don't know,' he said, in answer. Not very helpful.

'You must have some idea,' I said. 'Just an approximate figure.' I felt that since I'd made the initial gaffe I might as well press for some kind of answer.

'I have no idea,' he said. 'Why do you want to know?'

I hesitated. I didn't really know what to say. 'I was wondering what kind of role natural selection might have played in the colony's history,' I said, settling for the truth. 'If your population is very high or very low relative to the initial numbers of colonists it might offer some clue as to why this change has taken place – and what sort of effect it's having demographically.'

He shook his head. 'I'm sure the Planners will be able to supply you with the information you want,' he said. 'I have no knowledge of such things.'

Nathan, obviously wanting to heal the breach, said, 'You can't expect statistical information to be common knowledge, Taking census is an economic exercise, and there's probably not need for it yet. Have a little patience.'

I resented the patronising tone slightly, but I took the advice. I gathered my patience, and turned to look out of the window at the alien world which stretched from the roadside into the distance.

There was, after all, plenty of time.

CHAPTER FOUR

When we reached South Bay, Jason got out of the carriage and asked us to wait while he attended to some business. We asked what time the train was scheduled to leave and were informed that we had 'some time' in hand. When Nathan told him that we would look around the town, he seemed a fraction reluctant to sanction such a course of action, but there were no reasonable grounds on which he could refuse. He offered us the services of the man who had accompanied the coach on horseback as a guide. As a guide, however, the man – whose name was Lucas – was a complete washout. He seemed to be unnaturally taciturn. I don't believe that he was actually working hard to keep all information to himself – it seemed to come naturally to him.

We did discover, however, that the township had two primary roles to play in the colony. It was the southeasterly terminal of the railroad and began the distribution of most of the agricultural produce of the surrounding area. It was also a minor port, being situated in a bay between two large promontories. The major port, Leander, was away to the northwest. The greater importance of Leander was obvious in the fact that it had a deliberately conferred name rather than a title derived from a geographical or functional description.

South Bay had no beach. The waters of the ocean washed a shore which looked more like a river bank than a sea front. There were, of course, no tides to speak of on moonless Floria, and the promontories sheltered the harbour from violent weather. The sea was rippled by the wind, but only gently, and the water in the bay seemed extremely placid. The harbour itself had been cleared of weed, but farther out we could see the tips of the fronds which formed thick underwater forests in shallow water. Farther out to sea, I knew, vast rafts of floating weed could form, and the oceans of Floria were akin to the legendary Sargasso Sea of Earth – somewhat hazardous to navigate.

The ships moored in the harbour were all fairly small. None was longer than a hundred and fifty feet. They were wide bellied and looked sluggish. They were mostly cargo vessels. There were no fish in the sea, and though there was abundant invertebrate life the weed made netting virtually impossible, and the creatures were often so spectacularly ugly that there could be little demand for their meat.

Nathan asked Lucas about the extent of the exploration carried out by the colonists. How much did they know about conditions on other continents? How often were trans-oceanic trips made? Had the globe been circumnavigated? Were there any plans for subcolonies? When Lucas failed to provide adequate answers to these queries, merely indicating that ships *had* set out on voyages of exploration, Nathan grew a little impatient. The reason for Lucas's ignorance (or professed ignorance) was unclear. Was the distribution of knowledge in the colony really so parsimonious? Were the Planners maintaining a rigid control of information in order to secure their influence over the development of the colony? Or was Lucas simply not interested in the world beyond the horizon?

We watched the people working on the wharf, and there seemed to be activity enough to suggest that life was any-thing but listless. The big warehouses along the docks were busy, with goods being packed, loaded, and unloaded in an unsteady stream. There seemed to be little dogged efficiency about the way the men worked, but their effort was un-stinted. It was testimony, of a sort, to the health and success of the growing colony. I studied the range of size exhibited by the population. The men ranged from six feet five or so to some inches over seven feet. We saw fewer women, but they seemed to fall into a similar spectrum ranging from six feet to seven. Most seemed to have a build appropriate to their height, but I saw several people who looked perceptibly overweight. There were too few children and old people to allow generalisations – in fact, I saw only one or two indi-viduals who might have been over fifty, which might be evi-dence for the logical assumption that larger bodies have shorter life-expectancies.

Nathan and I attracted a good deal of curious attention. We must have seemed strange indeed to people who knew nothing of our provenance: ridiculous midgets wearing exotic clothing. Their own clothing was, by our standards, elaborate and dull in colour. We wore fewer, lighter, more efficient, and more colourful outfits. Nathan did not attempt to approach any of them in search of information or polite conversation. He was content to watch them overtly while they watched us – covertly, for the most part.

In the streets which led to the waterfront there was no less activity. Cobblers, carpenters, sailmakers, and other more specialised practitioners maintained workshops close to the shore, and few such businesses seemed to be in the doldrums. We saw some transactions taking place, where the money that changed hands appeared to be unstandardised coins whose value was assessed by the weight and species of metal involved. It was a rough and ready system, but exchange value was obviously identical to actual value – anyone could strike his own coins, provided that he first found and extracted the metal from its ore. The sophistications of bureaucratic economics were still to come here on Floria, although conditions already seemed ripe. Again, I was disposed to wonder, whether the Planners might not be wisely postponing the evil day as long as possible.

Both Nathan and I wanted to walk as far as possible in the time available – to see whatever might be around to be seen. Our walk took us through the town and beyond, and we ended up on the northern side of the bay looking back from the slope of the headland. Lucas had fallen behind and when we stopped he simply loitered forty or fifty yards away, making no attempt to join us. This gave us a chance to talk to one another without worrying about his hearing things not meant for his ears as well as sparing him our questions.

'Jason doesn't like us,' I said.

'He's wary of us,' Nathan replied. 'Wouldn't you be, in his place? He doesn't understand us. To him, Earth is just a name ... hardly a real place at all. The colony project, to him, is like a creation myth – it may be true but not really

55

relevant to the everyday business of living. The farmers were impressed – he's not. He's shrewd, hard-headed.'

'And maybe dangerous,' I added.

'That's *not* the right attitude,' he said.

Patronising bastard, I thought, and said, 'I don't like him.'

'Hostility,' he said, 'is the last thing we need. You don't have to like him – provided that you treat him like a favoured son.'

I thought, briefly and bitterly, *You should see the way I treat my son*. But I didn't say anything at all. I looked out over the bay, thinking about how beautiful it looked. If you like that sort of thing. I could see, albeit dimly, the great forest of weed which stretched away from the arms of the headlands out towards the horizon. The water was clear, and I could make out a profusion of colours which one only associates with tropical waters on Earth. Beneath a watery surface the photosynthetic optima are different, and browns and reds outweigh the greens.

Nathan seemed to feel that I'd been less than diplomatic. He still wanted to talk.

'Why are there no fish?' he asked, his gaze following the direction of mine. 'How is it that the whole evolutionary process was short-circuited here?'

I sat down on the slope, feeling the alien grass with the palms of my hands.

'It wasn't,' I said. 'We think the vertebrates are the most important part of the tree of life, but we're biased. Plant evolution here has been complex and the plants have reached a very high degree of sophistication. They're not the same kind of plants we find on Earth because their evolution hasn't been so drastically affected by the parallel evolution of certain types of animal, but it hasn't been short-circuited. And I wouldn't think that that would be an apt term to use in connection with the animal evolution either.'

I paused, and thought, *Who's being patronising now?*

'Basically,' I continued, 'there are two reasons why animal life here didn't develop in the same way that it did on Earth. There's no moon. No moon, no tides. No tides, no littoral

56

zone. Evolution begins in the sea, and the type of organism which eventually comes out of the sea on to the land depends very much on the manner of its coming out. On Earth, the borderland between the two environments is a regime of constant, cyclic change. Creatures living there evolve to cope with successive immersion and desiccation. The littoral zone not only provides a way station for creatures to develop ways of coping without the ocean, first temporarily and then permanently, it also makes creatures individually adaptable. Earthly animals are built to cope with change – all the invaders of the land on Earth were already highly sophisticated organisms when they said goodbye to the tidal zone and went in for full-time life on land. They had to be, because they'd come out by a difficult route, a regime in which natural selection was very strong, permitting rapid, diversifying evolution.

'But that didn't happen here. Here, there was no such way station, no regime of rigorous selection. Without rigorous selection, evolution remains much more subject to the dictates of chance. Land-forms did eventually arise, but they weren't super-refined in form and function. They weren't selected for individual adaptability. They're all worms and soft, squashy things. Once having opted for the land they've evolved ways of coping with desiccation, but they almost all remain creatures adapted to easy ways of life. Few of them eat one another – because there's an abundant supply of plants. Most of them don't even eat healthy plants, but specialise in rotting ones.'

'That covers land animals,' said Nathan, 'but what about fish?'

'I said there were two reasons,' I reminded him. 'No tides is one. The other is a corollary of that. You see it before you, as far as the eye can see.'

He found no immediate enlightenment in the ranging of his gaze.

'Weed,' I said. 'The absence of tides also means that the sea itself is a relatively static environment, and the plant life which evolved there took advantage of that fact. The shallows get clogged with anchored weed. In deeper waters,

57

floating weed occupies the surface and rotting vegetation the ocean floor, with a lifeless chasm in between. There's lots of scope for animal life – of certain kinds. The scavengers who move about the bottom, the worms, the things with the texture of jelly. But there are no openings for muscular, free-ranging swimmers. And again, it's all too easy for the scavengers because the plants produce so much. There are no incentives for animal-eating animals to evolve. The struggle for existence just isn't all that much of a struggle. In a billion years, maybe, things would have been different ... but even then, one wouldn't expect a regime of slow, steady change to produce the same kind of organisms as a regime of quick, cyclic change, even given twice as long.

'You know, Nathan, we don't realise how much we owe to that absurdly large moon of ours. If it wasn't for that freak, you and I wouldn't be here. And nor would the colonies ... because we'd never have found so many worlds where men can live but where no creatures comparable to man have evolved. Floria is just the extreme case: it's not coincidence that all the other colony worlds are worlds with moons conspicuously smaller than Earth's. And if we ever find another world in the right orbit, with a companion as big as the moon, *that's* where we can expect to find the guys who are going to give us trouble – or, if you look at it the other way, the guys who are going to provide us with stimulating conversation and rewarding partnership while we explore the universe together.'

'But there is intelligent life on some of the colony worlds,' he objected.

'Intelligent,' I agreed, 'but not similar. There's no conflict or contact ... and with all due respect to Mariel I don't believe there ever will be. Those aliens really *are* alien, in mind and in body. Their minds are structured to a wholly different range of priorities. Sure, some of them look like the idiots in plastic suits who used to feature in the old movies ... but that doesn't mean to say that there are metaphorical men wrapped up inside them just aching to come out for a cheeseburger, a chat, and a game of chess. They're not only

58

stranger than we think, but maybe stranger than we could ever imagine, and we'll need more than a fully certified Alice in Wonderland to get close to them.'

'You're pretty hard on Mariel,' he said.

'And this trip could be bloody hard on her,' I said. 'That gift of hers may be just enough to let them turn her adolescent mind inside out . . . and I don't mean that in any trivial sense. I mean *completely* crazy.'

'Did you talk to Pietrasante about that?' he wanted to know.

'Did I get the chance?' I said bitterly. 'Oh no! They were too worried about hurting my feelings to let me in on their plans. Nobody told me a damn thing until it was all worked out – in *committee* – and unchangeable.' I used *committee* as if it were a dirty word. Earth is run by committees. It has been for two hundred years. That's why it's in a mess, always has been, and always will be. The worst of it is that the alternatives are probably worse. Dictators are not nice. Sometimes, in thinking of my son and his faith, I almost wish I could believe in God myself, but I always run up against the problem of whether a God one can believe in would be a committee or a dictator. I wonder if the papal triumvirate has ever debated the issue.

Nathan changed the subject. It didn't seem worth pursuing when we had a different set of problems on hand immediately. 'If conditions here could never lead to the evolution of anything *like* man,' he mused, 'doesn't that imply a certain implicit hostility to human habitation? Or at least a certain inhospitality?'

'No,' I said comprehensively.

'Why not?'

'Because the colonists came here wanting to *use* the world, not to become adapted to it. Adaptation is a double-edged sword. When man moves into an ecosystem he fits too well he finds natural enemies – and where there are no natural enemies to start with it doesn't take long for them to turn up. Exploitation can run both ways. But not necessarily. Here, we have a high degree of chemical similarity between the

59

life-systems, but little organisational similarity. It should be possible for man – as a clever and superadaptable species – to exploit without being exploited.'

'And yet,' said Nathan, 'the people have changed, and are changing, in response to some factor in the environment here.'

'True,' I said. 'Puzzling, isn't it?'

He didn't seem to consider this an overwhelmingly successful reply. There are too many men who think that they can turn to an expert and say, 'This is your area of concern, what's the answer?' Nobody's omniscient.

Lucas, who'd been content to keep his distance until now, came up to us and informed us that it was time to start back. He didn't say how he knew, but we were prepared to trust his judgment.

This time, instead of lagging behind, our so-called guide led the way. He didn't believe in dawdling, it seemed, and because of his size his stride perpetually attempted to carry him on ahead of us. Every few paces, he had to pause to let us catch up, and it began to seem as if he had made a mistake in thinking we had adequate time by assuming that we could cover the same distance he could in the same kind of time.

Nathan made some attempt to keep up with him, but I was a little less ready to hurry so ostentatiously. Thus, as we walked, we tended to be perpetually strung out, with me to the rear.

As there was no conversation, and we were retracing ground we had already covered, I allowed myself to lose myself slightly in my thoughts. Thus, when I glanced up and saw something terrible about to happen my brain was too far behind my senses to make any immediate sense out of it. I didn't get to shout a warning.

From the loft of a warehouse ahead of us there extended a heavy wooden beam, pivoted within and equipped with block and tackle for lifting and shifting heavy goods from the cobblestones of the wharf. Leaning out from the loft was a man, holding by one hand the edge of a heavy net of rope, the rest of which was draped over the beam. He had only to flip his wrist to drop the net – and that was exactly what he did, just as Lucas was passing underneath. At that particular moment Nathan was trying to draw abreast of him, and he, too, was caught by the folds of the net and felled.

I stopped dead in my tracks, openmouthed. It seemed so obvious that it had been done on purpose – and so ridiculous that anyone should do such a thing. I stared helplessly while Lucas tried to rise, struggling fruitlessly with the tangled mass of the net.

Then something hit the back of my head like a sledge-hammer, and my thoughts imploded.

CHAPTER FIVE

I drifted slowly into a dream of intolerable pain. I seemed to be shot through and through with bolts of agonising force, confined and constrained as if my skull were *squeezing* my brain. I was dangling, helpless as a puppet, trapped in my body while the fire consumed me.

The dream slowly dissolved in returning consciousness.

The reality did not seem, at first, to be very much better. As the minutes ebbed by, however, I discovered that I was more or less intact. The pain in my head was fierce, but by no means intolerable. The sensations of confinement, of helpless dangling within the borderlands of self-awareness, slowly evaporated.

Long minutes passed while I could not find the energy to open my eyes or move my body.

I heard someone say, 'He's awake,' before I was conscious of having given any evidence of the fact. I heard footfalls, and then felt fingers gripping my jaw lightly. My head was turned for me. I opened my eyes wider.

He balanced my head so that I was looking up into his face. It was a face I'd seen before – a hundred times or more. On the wharf, in the streets of the town, back in the village.

Wherever I went for the rest of my life I would always know the swollen face of a Florian. The face had few characteristics to set it aside from others like it. It wasn't Jason.

I didn't say anything. I just bathed in the waves of my headache.

He turned away, briefly, and nodded to someone else. I heard a door close. Then he helped me sit up. There was a cup of water waiting on a small table beside the bed, and he put it to my lips. I took it off him – I wasn't *that* helpless. I took the water in small sips. I couldn't drain the cup because tilting my head back hurt too much.

I studied his face, carefully. He didn't quite have the same strong-man aura as the rest. His beard was trimmed into a neat triangle. It wasn't long since he'd last washed his face. He was paler than most, and smoother. An indoor man. Even Jason had had the look of a man who got about a lot. This was the first Florian I'd seen who was a desk man. I looked at his hands, and found that they were worn, but only slightly. Here, on a world where virtually every man might be expected to get through a fair amount of manual labour, was a teller instead of a doer. A man who gave orders.

He was smiling.

'Did you have to hit me so bloody *hard*?' I demanded.

'It wasn't me,' he answered, with a hint of irony. 'And it wasn't hard. But he's used to hitting men with thicker skulls.'

'He makes a habit of it, then?' I commented dryly.

'In the course of his work,' he said. He was still smiling. I was getting tired of people who smiled when there was nothing to smile about.

'Why did you have to hit me at all?' I asked. 'I'm a reasonable man. You could have tapped me on the shoulder and issued an invitation. Or were you upset because we didn't all walk under your net at once?'

'The essence of the manoeuvre,' he said, 'was speed. We had to remove you from the scene quickly and quietly. Before anyone had time to realise what had happened.'

'Why?' I asked bluntly. I felt that it was time to get to the heart of the matter. He hesitated, obviously wondering how much he ought to tell me. I looked around the room. There wasn't much to see. There were no windows, and there was no furniture except for the bed, the small table, and the stool that the big man was sitting on. There was an oil lamp on a bracket providing a wan yellow light. Nothing else.

'I wanted to talk to you,' he said, finally settling for telling me nothing – yet.

'Who are you?' I said.

'My name's Carl Vulgan,' he said. 'What's yours?'

'Alexis Alexander,' I said. 'Late of planet Earth. I presume that's what you want to talk about?'

'I'd like to know why you came to Floria,' he agreed.

'And I'd like to know why you want to know,' I countered.

He stopped smiling, but he wasn't angry or impatient. He seemed to think he had lots of time. 'You're the one who just dropped out of the sky,' he said. 'You're the one without the invitation. This is my world. Aren't I entitled to an explanation of why you've come?'

I shrugged. 'It's no secret,' I said. 'Earth is recontacting the colonies. The *Daedalus* – that's the ship – is fitted out as a laboratory. The general idea is that we can help you sort out any problems you're having with the alien life-system.'

'And what do you want in return?' he asked bluntly.

'We haven't come to collect taxes,' I assured him, in a sarcastic tone. 'We can't carry anything away with us. All we want to to do is help you and reopen a channel of communication between Floria and Earth. *Now* will you tell me what you're playing at? And where's Nathan?'

'Your companion is still with Jason,' he said.

'I saw you drop the net on him.'

'The net was to tangle things up while we got you away. We couldn't snatch both of you or Jason would expend twice as much effort looking for you. While he has one of you still in his tender care he has other priorities. We have, so to speak, equalised the situation. Attained a fairer distribution of visitors from outer space, if you wish.'

It was difficult to think with my head still throbbing, but I tried hard. Jason was taking us to the Planners, who controlled the colony but without wielding any real executive power. Vulgan looked like a man with executive power. Possibly, then, he represented the civil authority ... the metaphorical throne rather than the power behind it. He had taken me away from Jason, but had tried to make sure that Jason couldn't know who it was had taken me. Presumably, then, Jason and the Planners would not approve of Vulgan and whoever he represented making their own independent contact with us. There seemed to be a division of interests, perhaps a political conflict.

'Perhaps you don't realise,' he continued, when I didn't say anything, 'that your arrival here is a momentous event. It may be a critical point in our history. You must forgive us if our actions are a little hasty – certainly unrehearsed. We had not anticipated such a thing. We are, of course, delighted to see you, and we regret the rough handling. It was, unfortunately, necessary.'

'Because you didn't want us to go straight to the Planners and negotiate with them,' I guessed. 'You want us to negotiate with you. You want to use us to liberate you from the dictates of the Planners, whereas they would want to use us to help them maintain the status quo.'

'You seem to have grasped the basic situation,' he admitted – rather grudgingly. I think he was wondering how much Jason had told us while we were in the coach, and how much we might have learned from the villagers. It appeared that we had arrived at a bad moment, and set down squarely in the middle of a power struggle. Up to now, it had probably been conducted behind the scenes ... but our arrival might well bring it out into the open. When it comes to kidnapping people like pawns in a chess game trouble is just about to start boiling over.

'How did you know we'd landed?' I asked.

'A messenger from the village came to us last night,' he replied, no longer prevaricating. 'We were all set to welcome you with open arms when you came in on a farm cart. But you didn't. Jason got to you first.'

I was surprised. I tried to sit up, and found that the pain was now so dull that I could manage it. I felt a slight twinge of nausea.

'But if the messenger came to you,' I said, 'how did Jason know?'

'That,' said Vulgan, 'is one of the things *I* want to know.'

I had assumed, naturally enough, that Jason had come to meet us because of the messenger. Apparently, he had not. That opened up a number of questions. I realised that I had been assuming, without any good reason, that Jason was the proper authority, and Vulgan was the one trying to get in on the game. Now, I discarded that assumption along with the notion that 'proper authority' could mean anything at all. There were two sides playing, but who was right and who was wrong wasn't my business. I rubbed the back of my neck and wondered what the hell I was supposed to do in a situation like this. It hadn't been mentioned in the briefings – not, at any rate, the ones I'd been to. Nathan was the diplomat. I couldn't help thinking, rather ruefully, that the fools had snatched the wrong man. I wished that Nathan had my headache.

'Your political squabbles aren't our affair,' I said. 'We didn't come here in order to be pawns in your attempts to swing the balance of power about. We came to help ... to help all of you ... with problems that are much more elementary.'

'Aren't you a little *late* for that?' he said quietly. 'If we'd really found any serious problems in adapting to this world we'd all be dead by now. Our great-great-grandfathers would have perished in the attempt to make a living here.'

'We're late,' I agreed. 'Earth has her problems – and they're the same problems she always had. The political climate has been wintry for a long time with regard to interstellar travel. It's expensive, and being under the aegis of various international organisations its funding is affected by all kinds of factors. It only takes one major power to withdraw support, and then they all do ... and it takes one hell of a long time to put Humpty Dumpty back together again. But now, if all goes well, we can start again. We're late, but we've already arrived in time to help other colonies.'

I didn't mention that Kilner had arrived *too* late on one occasion. It didn't seem to be the right moment for total honesty, which is always the second best policy, if politicans are to be believed.

'But we have no problems,' said Vulgan.

'You think you don't,' I said. 'But I'm not convinced.'

He got up from the stool and took a pace or two away into the room. Then he turned back. He appeared to be doing some hard thinking.

'Earth has her problems,' he said, echoing my words as he considered them. 'International disputes ... but now things are getting back together again. ...'

'That's right,' I said helpfully.

'You've done this before?' he asked. 'Visited other colonies, that is.'

'Not personally,' I admitted. 'But the ship has. Four colonies have already been recontacted.'

'And they needed help? They had basic problems affecting the viability of the colony, and your personnel helped put things right?'

'Yes,' I said, feeling that perhaps we were getting somewhere.

'How was the help received?' he asked. 'Did *they* welcome you with open arms?'

'They thought we were late as well,' I admitted. 'They were rather bitter.'

'But we're different,' he said. 'We're successful. We've established ourselves here. We're building a new world. Left to ourselves, we can make a better world than Earth ... perhaps.'

My optimism was evaporating. Mariel had assured me that the farmers were sincere in making us welcome. They harboured no resentment, like the men of Kilner's colonies. They had done well, and they didn't feel that they had been abandoned. All well and good.

But ...

From the viewpoint of the men on top in this society things looked different. They didn't hate us, either. They didn't feel abandoned. They were *glad* they'd been left alone to get on with it. They *wanted* to be left alone to get on with it. So far as they were concerned, renewed contact with

66

Earth was something they reckoned they needed like a hole in the head. They wanted to look after their own garden, and grow it their way. OK, they were in dispute among themselves as to who was to plot a course through the stormy seas of history . . . one man's Utopia is another man's poison and no politican likes being a puppet, especially for an island colony of intellectuals. But Vulgan and the Planners could have at least one thing in common. They wouldn't want recontact, except – perhaps – on their own rigorous terms.

'We can help you,' I said, feeling that it was necessary to insist.

'And what do you want in return?' he demanded.

I just couldn't say 'Nothing'. For one thing, it sounded too facile for a man like Vulgan to believe. For another, I wasn't sure in my own mind that it was true. There was a lot more to the politics that lay behind the reinstitution of the space programme than I knew about. I was only a worker, hired for a job. *I* believed that space travel was vital to the future of mankind, but somehow I just couldn't see Nico Pietrasante thinking the same way. If he had persuaded the wayward members of the UN to start contributing to space travel again, said this small cynical voice, then he's promised them that they'll get something out of it.

'What we want is to restore communication,' I said. 'Establish some kind of connection between the scattered human worlds.'

He wasn't overly impressed by this statement. He didn't seem to think that it was a real answer to his question.

It wasn't.

'We don't need communication,' he said. 'We don't need help.'

'That's what everyone says,' I protested. 'But you just don't realise . . . what you see as normal isn't necessarily inconsequential. The giantism which is universal here seems normal to you, but very strange to me. It sometimes take an outsider's judgment to expose and analyse problems before they become acute. There are questions which need answers before we can tell whether you have problems or not. How many people are there in the colony . . .?'

I had been meaning to go on and pose more simple questions, but I stopped as I saw him react to that one. His face didn't change as much as Jason's had, but a definite look of suspicion came into his eyes. I realised suddenly – perhaps belatedly – why it seemed to them to be so significant.

The first colony ships had arrived here a hundred and eighty years ago, and more had come over a period of forty years or so. Then they had stopped. Since then, Floria had never seen a starship. And now ... recontact. From their point of view, recontact meant one thing above all others. More colonists. More ships, delivering immigrants by the thousand into their world: the world they had sweated to build.

They saw us as the advance guard of an invasion.

And they didn't want that.

Maybe it was a threat that existed only in their own minds. Maybe not, if this colony really was as successful as it seemed. Either way, it was a threat they would take very seriously indeed. And to prevent it happening – if they came to believe that it *might* prevent it happening – they might be only too ready to kill us all. I realised for the first time the depth of the trouble I was in.

CHAPTER SIX

What now? I wondered.

I felt suddenly afraid, but I didn't know what I was supposed to be doing. Should I try to escape – to get back to the ship and hole up? That was hardly what we'd come for. We had come to open communications – it was up to us to start communicating. If the Florians didn't want us, it was up to us to show them that they needed us. And it was up to us to show them what a terrible mistake it would be on their part to take hostile action against us.

I remembered the riders I had seen when Jason's coach had come to meet us. Perhaps they – someone – had already made a move against the ship. Maybe I wasn't the only prisoner, by now.

I knew they couldn't take the ship. That was impossible. At the first hint of trouble Rolving would seal it tight, and neither threat nor persuasion could make him open it up. It was impregnable to any means of force the colonists might care to try against it. If necessary, Pete Rolving could fly it home alone – and standing orders would ensure that at least one other person would be with him. Standing orders would also ensure that he *would* fly it back alone, abandoning the rest of us, if things got too hot.

The ship *had* to be invulnerable. And by the same logic, its personnel on the ground had to be totally vulnerable. We were, whether we liked it or not, at the mercy of the people of any world we contacted. We came to talk and to offer help. We brought no gifts and we carried no weapons. We, ourselves, were the whole message. We had to be vulnerable to make it clear that we came in good faith.

I continued to knead the back of my neck with my right hand, hoping that the pain would go away. I realised that it was no good flogging my brain. 'What now?' wasn't my question at all. It was Vulgan's. The ball was in his court.

He was still standing a couple of yards away, waiting. I eyed him apprehensively.

'Do you want something to eat?' he asked. It was a friendly question. I think he was trying to patch things up. He didn't want me as an enemy ... not yet.

I shook my head, with some difficulty. 'I had a big breakfast,' I said dryly.

'That was some time ago,' he said.

'Yesterday?'

He grinned, showing a lot of teeth. 'You weren't out that long.'

'I don't feel like eating right now,' I said.

'Are they all as small as you on Earth?' he asked, suddenly feeling free to indulge a little harmless curiosity.

'Smaller,' I said. 'I'm a tall man.'

He nodded, to show that I was confirming what he already knew.

'Everything here grows big,' he said. 'Horses, pigs, pigeons.' He was testing out the assertion, waiting to see whether I'd agree with it. Horses I'd seen, and pigs, but pigeons were something I hadn't thought of. It made sense, of course, that they'd have imported Earthly birds – it's easy to carry eggs, but there was one aspect of that which hadn't occurred to me.

'Your pigeons,' I said pensively. 'Can they fly?'

'No,' he said, genuinely surprised.

'Can *any* of your birds fly?'

He shook his head.

It made sense. A man grows an extra ten per cent and becomes a strong man. But a bird grows ten per cent and never gets off the ground again. Being big isn't all good. It didn't matter, of course, to the birds. There was nothing to fly away from, here. And then I remembered that it wasn't just carnivores that were missing from Floria's ecosystem. There was not a single flying creature. Not a bird, not a bee, not a tiny fly. Why? Because there was no incentive to fly? Or because if you're going to be a flyer you have to be able to stay slim? On Floria, said Vulgan, *everything* grew big.

'It's all very well,' I told him, 'to say with pride that everything here grows big. But pride, as someone once said, goeth before destruction.'

He didn't get the message. I didn't expect him to. The little guy who walks around in a world of giants saying 'Small is best' is never likely to get much of an audience. People tend to suspect his motives.

'Never mind,' I said. 'What happens next?'

By now, he'd made up his mind.

'I'm going to take you to the capital,' he said. 'I can't keep it from Jason's ears that I've got you, so I'll have to make use of you. We're going to see Ellerich.'

'Who's he?'

'The Colony Manager. In name only.'

'But he has ambitions?'

Vulgan didn't reply to that one.

'How do you propose to get me there?' I asked.

'By train.'

'Won't Jason try to get me back?'

He shook his head. 'We aren't afraid of that. If he'd known for certain where you were after we removed you from Lucas's care, he might have come to get you ... if he thought he could get away with it. But he'll be on the island by now. By the time word gets back to him that you're on the train with a police escort *everybody* will know who and where you are. We'll be in the open – committed, if you like – but you'll be safe with us.'

'A police escort?' I queried.

He grinned again. 'The man who hit you was one of my men,' he said. 'I'm the chief of police here in South Bay.'

By this time, I didn't find that news altogether surprising.

'Wouldn't it have been easier to arrest us all? Jason, Lucas, Nathan, me ... and all so much tidier? If you're the law why do you need the cloak and dagger?'

'Jason is above the law,' he said simply. 'That's the whole problem. That's one of the reasons we want things changed.'

'I see,' I said. Florian politics sounded depressingly like politics back home. I recalled again the adage about people who lack respect for history.

I went with him out of the cell and upstairs into the main hall of the police station. He asked me again whether I wanted any food, and again I refused. He left me sitting to one side while he talked to a group of men in dark brown uniforms. I eyed the door speculatively while this was going on, calculating my chances in a sudden sprint. I figured I would win, but staging a bold escape is only a good idea when you have somewhere to run *to*. Once outside, I had no chance of mingling with the crowds, and there was no one who was likely to help me get back to the ship in spite of police, Planners, and all other interested parties. I shelved the idea of taking melodramatic action, though I still felt that I ought to be looking for something constructive to do instead of surrendering meekly to the dictates of other people.

It proved to be only a short walk from the police station to the railway station. My police escort consisted of Vulgan and two uniformed men. They gave me a heavy coat which added considerably to my bulk, but they didn't explain whether it was an attempt to make me less conspicuous or a gesture of goodwill in case the night was exceptionally cold. To them, I suppose, my light clothing must seem inapt for a temperate climate, although it was, in fact, quite warm.

They hustled me along through ill-lit streets, but made no real attempt to hide me. The last vestiges of twilight were dying, but not all the street lamps had been lit. They appeared to be oil lamps, and I assumed that this must be the standard mode of illumination throughout the colony until I reached the station, which was more brightly lit by a mixture of lamps and electric light bulbs. Obviously the Planners did not mean to restrict technology too strictly, although they seemed to be rather cautious in letting it out.

I caught barely a glance of the locomotive as I was bundled into a passenger coach at the rear of the train, but it seemed by far and away the most impressive machine I had so far seen on Floria. It was a great black monster of a steam locomotive, seething noisily as it prepared to begin its journey, making itself heard even above a constant clatter of goods being moved in and out of the station. The platform itself was clear – the train was all set to go.

The carriage was divided into separate compartments, but these contained only seats – the total length of the track was probably not more than a few hundred miles and sleeping accommodation was likely to be a luxury for which there was little enough demand.

I took a window seat, but one of the policemen reached across me to pull down a blind. When I put out a hand to stop him he turned to check with Vulgan. The chief of police shrugged, and the blind stayed up. It was only a matter of moments, though, before the train began to pull out of the station and into the gathering night, where there was nothing to be seen except reflections of the carriage's interior.

I made myself more comfortable in the seat, taking off the

large coat and putting it beside me. Vulgan sat opposite, and the two men in uniform flanked the door.

'How long will it take?' I asked automatically – realising as I said it that I might only get yet another vague answer. But railways have timetables, and so do policemen.

'A hundred and eighty minutes,' he said.

I did a quick conversion in my head. Floria's day was about ten per cent shorter than Earth's, and the colonists presumably used metric hours – ten to a day and a hundred minutes to the hour. A hundred and eighty Florian minutes would be about two hundred and thirty Earth minutes. Four hours.

'That's to Leander,' added Vuglan unhelpfully. 'We won't get to the capital until tomorrow midday. There's a two-hour wait in Leander . . . you'll be able to get some sleep.'

And, I thought, if anyone *is* going to start trouble, that's when and where . . .

'And then?' I said. 'You still haven't told me what you want me *for*.'

'If you're going to be making deals with anyone on this world,' he said, 'you make them with us. With Ellerich and the civil authorities. Not with the Planners. That's *if* we can work out any kind of deal at all.'

'And if not?' I asked, feeling that it just wasn't worth trying to hammer it into his skull that we weren't looking for a deal, at least not in his sense of the word.

'We'll decide that when the time comes.'

'And what happens in the meantime?' I asked. 'While you're talking to me and the Planners are talking to Nathan?'

'We'll sort out our own troubles for the time being,' he said.

He was being so dogmatically stupid that I just had to tell him. 'You snatched the wrong man,' I said. 'Nathan Parrick is the man with the power to negotiate. 'I'm just a biologist. It's my job to run the lab, to observe, to investigate. If anyone in our group can speak for the UN, it's Nathan. Not me. You picked the wrong midget, friend.'

He stared at me hard. He didn't seem at all upset by the

revelation. 'You're what we've got,' he said simply. 'We'll tell you what we want – it's up to you to make the rest of your party see sense.'

'I don't think there's any way any of us can see the sense of your starting a civil war here, with us in the middle,' I told him. 'What makes sense – at least as I see it – is for everyone to get together and talk. You and the Planners together. No cloak and dagger, no secrets.'

He glanced out of the window. We were on a long curve, travelling quite slowly. The train lurched slightly, and the click of the wheels as they passed the small gaps between the sections of rail were separate, measured like the ticking of an old clock. Slowly, though, they began to increase in frequency. It was as though time was speeding up as we came off the bend.

He turned back to me abruptly. 'Can you read, Mr Alexander?' he asked.

'Of course I can read.'

'Of *course* you can read,' he echoed. 'As it happens, so can I. But *he* can't, and neither can *he*.' Here he pointed to each of the uniformed men in turn. They were both watching him, soberly, pretending disinterest. 'Do you know *why* they can't read?' he finished.

'The Planners?' I said hesitantly.

'The Planners,' he echoed, in a firmer tone. 'In the minds of the planners, it is not only unnecessary for the mass of the population to be able to read, it is actually undesirable. Knowledge has to be under control, and you cannot control knowledge unless you can control the means of acquiring it. Every year, a handful of students go to the island to begin what the Planners consider to be an education. Nine out of every ten come back here, knowing just what the Planners think it good for them to know and just how the Planners think it ought to be applied. Those nine become civil servants, administrators, colony managers, chiefs of police. The tenth stays on the island to learn more – much more. To become, in fact, a Planner himself – or herself. To become the guardian of that which other men *must not* know, to

74

learn the secrets which have to be kept. Do you know what a gun is, Mr Alexander?'

'Yes,' I said warily.

'Tell me,' he said.

'It's a weapon,' I said uneasily.

'How does it work?'

I said nothing, but simply waited, unwilling to go on.

'Now there,' he said, 'you have a perfect example of the logic of the Planner. It is good to know ... but not to know too much. *I* know that a gun is a weapon, Mr Alexander. But I don't know how one works. I've never seen one. If any exist, on Floria, they are on the island. The Planners, I think, would prefer it if the word itself did not exist. Perhaps, someday, they will make it a crime to utter it. It is illogical, you see, to have a law which says "guns are forbidden" when no one to whom the law applies is permitted to know the meaning of the word. Far more orderly to dispense with the concept altogether. At the moment, they withhold only objects, and information. But it is only logical that they should also try to withhold ideas. You cannot control knowledge without controlling discovery, and you cannot control discovery without controlling thought, and when you control thought ... do you see what I'm getting at, Mr Alexander?'

'You don't like being manipulated by the Planners.'

He sighed. 'There's more *to* it than that, Mr Alexander. You know there is. It's not just the fact of manipulation, or the manner of the manipulation, but the whole philosophy that lies behind it. In the beginning, the Planners wanted to build a better world, to divert the course of history so that we wouldn't end up in the same mess as the Earth the original settlers left behind. But it's become more than that. The Planners are more than guides: they want to be gods, and they want us to be the clay they mould. We don't want that.'

'Sometimes,' I said carefully, 'I think Earth would be a much better place if no one knew what a gun was.'

'I don't know about Earth,' he said, in slightly tired tones. 'And I don't know about guns. But I know this. I do not want a law which forbids me to think and to know. If the law said "The *use* of guns is forbidden," then I might think it a good law. If I knew what a gun was, and how it *might* be used.'

'The trouble is,' I said, 'that once people know *how* to use a gun, there's no way of stopping them. You're a policeman. How many laws have never been broken because everyone feels that they're *good* laws? How many of the men in your cells are just rebels against injustice, and how many just want to get away with it?'

'You think the Planners are right?' he said, in a scathing voice.

I let a moment go by, and then I shook my head. 'No,' I said, 'I don't think they're right. but it doesn't make any difference. We didn't come here to take sides in *any* dispute. We can't. We have to deal with the colony as a whole. You must see that.'

He shook his head. 'I don't think the colony *is* a whole,' he said. 'Not anymore.'

And the ironic thing is, I thought, *that it seems to have been our arrival here that has opened the breach.*

CHAPTER SEVEN

After a time I managed to yield to the rhythm of the train, shutting out most of the noise and ignoring the occasional lurch. I dozed albeit very lightly. Periodically, when a strong tremor took hold of the carriage, or one of the others moved, I would open my eyes momentarily. In between such occasions, time slid by with liquid ease.

Vulgan remained alert, a long way from sleep, with his eyes always open, always moving, but the uniformed men both drifted off into sleep. I dreamed the casual dreams of semi-consciousness, bright and clear, but dissolving at the slightest pinprick of a conscious thought. The dreams seemed full of the problems of relative size: they were Gulliverian dreams in which I was confronted on the one hand by giants, and on the other by dwarfs. I was enmeshed, like Alice, in a looking-glass world where the absurdity of questions was exaggerated, and innocence made stupidity out of sophistication. Why can't pigeons fly? Why are giants? Who wants to be the white knight?

My body gained, if my mind did not. I needed the rest.

When I awoke, I found myself stretched out on the seat, with the coat draped over me like a blanket. I couldn't remember whether I had thus arranged myself, or whether Vulgan had assisted me into a more comfortable position. One of the uniformed men had gone, the other had been roused. Vulgan seemed not to have slept at all. The train was slowing down.

I looked out of the window. To the side of the train it was pitch-dark, but as I craned my neck to peer along the direction in which the train was travelling I saw clusters of light up ahead. The clicking of the wheels in the gaps between sections of rail was unsteady, like the rattling of dice in a cup.

'We're pulling into Leander,' he said.

'On time?' I asked.

'Almost,' he said. 'Relax. We'll get some food. Then more sleep.'

'Are we getting out?'

He shook his head. 'One of the men will report in,' he said. 'It will be better if we simply remain where we are.'

We cruised into the station, and gradually eased to a halt. The noise of the engine slowly died away, and the sounds of the station echoed hollowly in the relieved silence.

I looked out on to the platform. There were ten or a dozen men moving to the goods wagons which made up the bulk of the train. Obviously there was a certain amount of work to be done in exchanging cargo – that might be why there was such a long layover scheduled. Perhaps, too, we might pick up some early risers as passengers for the capital by the time we were all set to leave.

I watched a couple of people dismount from our carriage, stretch their limbs, shiver in the cold night air, and then begin to move off in the direction of the barriers thirty or forty yards up the platform. As my eyes followed them, I saw someone else – someone coming *from* the barriers.

It was Jason. Lucas was with him, and one other man. He was moving quite confidently and openly.

'You've got a visitor,' I said to Vulgan, with a note in my voice that was almost mockery.

He glanced out of the window, following the direction of the finger I pointed. When he looked back at me, his mouth was set hard. He just sat back and waited, saying nothing.

The second policeman came back into the compartment and offered the same news. Vulgan answered him with only a gesture, and the man sat down. When we heard footsteps coming along the corridor I was the only one who kept my eyes on the door.

It opened. Jason looked bigger, framed in the doorway, than he had before. He was noticeably more powerful than Vulgan. His mien seemed distinctly less pleasant. The folds of his face were glistening with a faint sweat despite the cold. His expression was slightly smug. Because I was the only one looking at him his gaze settled on me first.

'Hello, Mr Alexander,' he said.

I nodded bleakly.

He turned to Vulgan. 'It was good of you to locate our guest so quickly and bring him along,' he said smoothly. 'We're very grateful to you.'

I'm sure that for a moment or two Vulgan was really tempted to go along with the pretence. He was scared of Jason . . . it showed in his face. Perhaps, even now, it would have been easy for him to go back, to cancel out his actions and ambitions. For some reason, though, I didn't find myself wishing that he would. In fact, I was almost glad when he didn't. I didn't like Jason any more than he did.

'He's coming with me,' said the police chief. 'We're going to Hope Landing. It's Paul Ellerich that these people have come to see.'

Jason's eyes flickered from Vulgan to me and back again,

trying to gauge the degree of common cause which might exist between us. He had no way of knowing what Vulgan had told me, or how far my sympathies might have been seduced. I wondered how he'd known we would be on the train. He *had* known – this was no part of a large-scale search.

'This is a matter for the Planners,' said Jason. 'You know I have the necessary authority. You must allow Mr Alexander to come with me. Ellerich will be notified in due course ... he'll no doubt be summoned to the island.'

'This time,' said Vulgan levelly, 'the Planners will have to come to us.'

I watched them as they dragged their hostilities out from hiding. I could virtually hear them stacking up the odds in their minds, adding up the situation. Whatever happened after this, the battle had been joined, at least between these two. They were three against three, but there wasn't the slightest sign of any impending violence. Jason made no move to play it tough. It wasn't his way. I realised that the Planners might well have enjoyed a measure of success in changing or controlling the ways in which people habitually thought. Jason's counterpart on Earth would have reached for a gun, and the two cops might well have been waving theirs the moment the door opened. Neverthless, the atmosphere here didn't exactly strike me as civilised.

Jason still had cards to play. He looked at me again.

'I think you should come with me, Mr Alexander,' he said.

And suddenly, the ball was in my court. It really hadn't occurred to me until then that this might happen. I was lodged in my corner, waiting for the two giants to argue it out, winner take all. The idea that I might be called upon to choose simply hadn't entered into my choice. Vulgan couldn't keep me any more than Jason could take me away.

I hesitated, wondering if there was any way I could weigh the consequences of the alternatives. There didn't seem to be anything in standing orders to cover it, and I was damned if I was going to sit there and ask myself what Nathan Parrick would do if *he* were in my place.

I did the simplest thing. I asked, 'Why shouldI?'

'Vulgan is trying to use you,' Jason replied. 'He's trying to be an opportunist ... to further his own political ambitions. He's not acting in your interests, nor in the interests of the colony. I don't know what he's told you, but his real intention is to cause strife. It would be a bad mistake for you to allow yourself to be used.'

'Where's Nathan Parrick?' I asked.

'He went to the island this evening. He's with the Planners now. That's where you should be, too, Mr Alexander. You're a scientist. Your business is with the scientists of this world, not with the bureaucrats at Hope Landing. You have nothing in common with Vulgan. I know that he's an officer of the law, but you must surely have realised that it was an officer of the law who abducted you. Vulgan is no longer operating as a policemen but as a free agent.'

All of which sounded very true. Jason had a strong case. It was true that I didn't like him, but that prejudice was immaterial. It was my job to make contact, not to start civil wars.

Vulgan was watching me. He must have seen the decision in my face.

'Wait a minute,' he said. Then, to Jason, 'If your intention is to establish friendly and meaningful relations with these people, *why did your men attack their ship?*'

I didn't know whether Vulgan was guessing or whether he really knew. He must have had plenty of time before we left South Bay to send men out to the ship, and maybe they had returned – I didn't know what had passed while he was talking to the men in the station. But if it *was* a guess, it hit the mark.

Jason was suddenly lost in the confusion of trying to estimate how much Vulgan knew, how much I knew, and what interpretation we had put on events. What he finally said was, 'That's a lie.'

But I didn't believe him.

'Of course the Planners sent men to your ship,' he said quickly. 'We must establish a base in the village. But this accusation concerning an attack is nonsense.'

'You didn't say anything about that before,' I pointed out. '*We* told *you* that it would be necessary to establish a base near the ship, because it couldn't be moved. But you said nothing about men having already gone out there. When we met you on the road, I saw other riders in the distance – but you said nothing about them. The messenger Harwin sent into South Bay went to Vulgan, yet you let us believe that you came in response. How *did* you know the ship had landed?'

'The Planners have an elaborate information network,' he replied. 'We know everything that happens in the colony. Yes, the riders you saw *were* headed for your ship, and no, I didn't mention them. I was deliberately cautious. Wouldn't you have been, in my situation? I knew nothing about you – your purpose in coming here or the manner of your coming. I misled you. But I assure you that our intentions are in no way hostile. Your ship has not been attacked. Only *you* have been attacked. By Vulgan. He is the man who has exposed his determination to use you even if it means injuring you. Vulgan and Ellerich have no real understanding of the colony, the way it is organised, or the principles behind that organisation. Don't be misled by the title of "Colony Manager" or "Chief of Police" – these men are of minor importance carrying out routine work. If you want to know about this colony, if you want to do anything *for* this colony, the men you must talk to are the Planners.'

Again, I had to concede that his arguments had force. Maybe the ship had been attacked, maybe it hadn't. I *still* didn't trust Jason. But there were other priorities. We had to be vulnerable in order to carry out our alloted task. If the colonists attacked us, it was our job to be attacked, *not* to fight back. The old theory that it takes two to make a quarrel isn't necessarily so, but it certainly helps to avert a quarrel if one side is ready to capitulate first and argue later. But how many sides were there here?

I had a flash of inspiration, albeit not a bright one.

'Suppose we *all* go to the island,' I said. 'Let's *all* talk to the Planners.'

Vulgan didn't like the idea one little bit – and I hadn't expected him to. What surprised me, though, was the fact that Jason didn't appear to have the least enthusiasm for it either. Neither seemed to have heard that compromise is the soul of diplomacy.

There was a pause while both Vulgan and Jason looked at one another, each running possibilities quickly through his mind. It was awkward and there seemed, to judge by their faces, not the slightest hope of resolution. I was desperately afraid that despite the Planners this situation might ultimately lead to violence. Violence arises out of frustration, and both these men seemed very frustrated.

Why on Earth, I wondered, apologising to myself for the inaptness of the expression, *is Jason so horrified by the idea of Vulgan coming along?* My suspicious mind couldn't help thinking that it might be because something was scheduled to happen that Jason didn't want Vulgan to know about. . . .

And then there was a scream.

It was high-pitched, but it was undeniably a masculine scream. It contained rage, surprise, and a great deal of pain.

It broke up the tripartite impasse. Jason was the first to move towards the corridor, and Vulgan followed. At first, they moved fairly casually, motivated primarily by curiosity, but then someone shouted 'Arne!' in urgent tones.

Jason moved to the door at the end of the carriage with a litheness that seemed strange in one of his dimensions. I had managed to slip out of the compartment after Vulgan, before the two uniformed men, and I got down to the platform immediately behind the police chief, but several paces down on Jason.

This station was larger than the one at South Bay by a factor of three, and its layout was far more complex. Instead of being gathered tightly about a terminal the complex here was scattered about a through line with numerous sidings. There was a large apron of open concrete between the train and the bays to and from which the men were busy transferring loads. They had started on several trucks at once, and the platform was strewn with bales and boxes and wooden trolleys.

A man was lying on the platform some forty or fifty feet up the train, curled up and still moaning. One does not expect to see a man seven feet tall felled and moaning – nor, for that matter, does one expect to hear them scream – but on a world of such giants there is obviously not the same compulsion to live up to the image. They say that the bigger you are the harder you fall, and this one certainly seemed to have been laid out comprehensively.

No one was paying much attention to him. They were all looking up. I looked up, too, and saw who'd hit him. . . .

And she saw me. . . .

'Run!' she howled.

For a moment, I was rooted to the spot. The very last thing I'd expected to see was Karen Karelia, on top of a goods wagon, wielding a three-foot crowbar with a wicked hook at one end. That she was ready to use it was obvious. Her ankles, at least, were within the reach of the felled man's co-workers, but no one was attempting to grab her.

Perhaps it was as well that I was still for a second, because it allowed Vulgan to take an extra step forward, and so leave me, for the moment, alone and with the space to act.

When she shouted again, elaborating somewhat, 'Get out of here, you dumb bastard!' I was ready and able to comply. The two uniformed men were still behind me and would have had me if I'd tried to run back beyond the train, but there was one way that was unguarded. There was a gap between the carriage and the edge of the platform just big enough to take a long, thin body. Before anyone could stop me, I launched myself into it, and under the train. The best thing of all was that every damn one of them was too fat to follow.

I hauled myself up on to the far platform, and looked back for Karen. She was running along the top of the train in my direction, jumping the gaps between the trucks with some difficulty but without losing her balance. She came to the end of a sequence of half a dozen roofed trucks and then leaped down into an open wagon. Here, one of Jason's men made a serious attempt to get at her, and the blow she gave his fingers with the iron bar must have smashed his hand beyond repair. She came over the side of the wagon to the empty track on our side of the train and I extended a hand to help her up on to the platform.

Jason was coming over the same wagon behind her, and one of Vulgan's cops had gone back into the carriage and was now opening the door on the near side of the train. But we had five or six strides' start, and we took them at maximum speed. We raced towards the nearer end of the station – the south side, by which the train had come in. Beyond that there was a curtain of lovely darkness.

The only man who had a chance to stop us was a lone railway official who had, by an unfortunate stroke of fortune, been attending to some business down that end of the vacant platform. But as he saw us coming he made no move to cut us off, simply staring at us in blatant incomprehension. Jason yelled something at him, but even then he didn't immediately get into gear. The chance went by, and we ran out of the glare of the electric light and into the dismal night.

When a northbound railway line curves to go west you build the station at the southwest corner of town – and that, for us, was just about perfect. Beyond the station in the direction that we were going there was no town at all – merely a conglomeration of railroad sheds, and sidings containing spare trucks. There was no light to speak of and plenty of cover. There was no problem at all about shaking the pursuit. Giants may make great weight lifters but they aren't much at sprinting and no damn use at all at middle-distance running. Our big problem was keeping our feet on ground that was littered with junk just waiting to trip us up and break our ankles, but we were lucky. A couple of stumbles, but no falls. We made it through the yards and out into the open country, and once there it was all too easy to get well and truly lost.

CHAPTER EIGHT

We kept going for about an hour or so, picking our way carefully across country that was moderately open but very much up-and-down. We crossed a small stream and passed through a couple of small woods. We had only the stars to light our way and they weren't exactly trying as hard as they might have. The idea was to keep going until we hit some large region where we could hide out without fear of being cut off by any search – a forest, for preference. Where we wound up, though, was an area of steep slopes and exposed rocks where we either had to double back or go up into the hills. Here the territory was really rough – the rocks were weathered very unevenly and there were innumerable gullies and clefts hidden even from careful probing by dense vegetation. If we tried to go farther in the dark one of us would almost certainly have ended up with a serious injury, so we settled for searching out a comfortably claustrophobic crevice where we could rest.

Resting was not so easy. The adrenalin was surging in my blood, my head was ringing, and my breath was coming in ragged gulps. My whole being seemed to be vibrating with pain and effort. I slumped down with my backside on a cushion of damp mossy stuff and my back leaning against a near-vertical stone face, and tried hard to recover my breath. It took time.

Karen seemed to be the same way, but she found her voice first, even though she used it only to say, 'Hi.'

'What the hell are you doing here?' I asked, feeling that the time for amiable greetings was past.

'What the hell are *you*?' she countered.

'I was riding in the train,' I said, implying that of all the places on the planet I might have been, that was the most appropriate.

'So was I,' she said. 'Only I didn't have a ticket. I was in a truck.' She was still holding the hooked crowbar in her right

85

hand, and I could hear its point stirring the dirt between her feet.

I didn't bother to ask *why* she'd been in the truck. I just waited until she got around to it.

'You'd hardly been gone an hour,' she began, 'when things started happening back at the farm. A dozen riders came in and started behaving in a manner that seemed just a little high-handed. Linda was already back at the ship, but Mariel and I were looking around. We saw them before they saw us, and we listened while they were arguing with Saccone – the farmer. They seemed to be trying to move him out of his farm. A couple of them went to the ship. They weren't armed and they looked harmless enough except for being built like tanks.

'Mariel and I stayed out of sight, and we watched. Conrad came out of the lock to talk. We couldn't hear what was said, but it started out polite and slowly degenerated. I think they wanted in, and weren't too clever about providing reasons. When Conrad wouldn't let them, as per policy, they tried to jump him. They dragged him out of the lock and tried to get at the inner door. Pete must have released a whiff of gas because they both came back out in a hurry looking very tearful. Conrad took the opportunity to get back in, and though he probably got sick doing it he's maybe in the best place.

'We had no chance. They were already looking for us, and while we'd been watching the fun they'd found us. We ran . . . but they got Mariel.'

'You left her?' I interposed.

'Sure. I left her. I can't see that dirty look you're giving me but wipe it off anyway. I figured I might be able to get her away if I could stay loose. . . . Oh, damn it, no I didn't. . . . We were both running when they got her. What was I supposed to do – stop and give up?'

'You *know* that's what you were supposed to do,' I said.

There was a moment's silence. 'Yeah,' she said finally. 'Well, I didn't. It seemed like a good idea at the time. This isn't like the type of situation they talked about when they briefed us on the tribulations of Kilner's crew. And it wasn't as if I were hauling out a gun and blasting. All I wanted to do was stay free, get out of the way. I didn't know who those guys were, but they didn't seem to me like representatives of the government. I mean, the villagers were friendly ... I thought everyone was friendly. It just threw me, that's all.

'Anyhow, I hiked east, because that's the way you'd gone – you and Nathan. I had some idea of catching up with you, joining you if things were OK, maybe helping you if things were sticky. It did occur to me that a planet is a big place, and that I was as inconspicuous as a ladybird in a beehive, but not until later. I hit the tracks, eventually, when it was just about getting dark, and I couldn't decide whether to walk along them into town or what. While I was thinking, along came the train. And I was on this bend, where it had to go slow, so ...'

'I bet you signed on for this trip looking for adventure.' I commented bitterly.

'Don't be so bloody smart,' she said. 'Where are you, hey?'

And that, of course, was true. Given the stimulus, I'd run just as she had. Admittedly, I'd been in an awkward spot, where following standing orders and meekly submitting to the demands of the natives involved certain difficulties, but the fact remained that I had done what came naturally ... and it had seemed like a good idea at the time.

'What about the incident at the station?' I asked.

'They were unloading my truck. The guy found me. He grabbed. What would you do if a seven-foot ... Oh, hell ... sure I should have surrendered meekly. "It's a fair cop," I should have said. Only it didn't seem fair, he wasn't a cop, and I didn't think his intentions were honourable. I was scared. I tried to fend him off and he got mad ...'

'So you belted him in the balls with the hooked end of an iron bar,' I finished. 'Defending your maidenly honour? In *this* day and age?'

'It isn't the twenty-third century here,' she muttered. 'More like the eighteenth. No, I wasn't afraid of rape ... just afraid, period. I hit him to get him out of the way so I could run.'

'Getting to be a habit, isn't it?' I said sourly.

'Isn't it?' she echoed. She didn't exactly sound contrite. She'd certainly sent all the sweet talking we'd done about contact and vulnerability to hell and gone. Maybe she'd cocked the whole operation. But what she'd done was only natural. Anyone might have done the same. Or why was I here? Like she said I wasn't sitting in the right place to be so bloody smart. I hadn't stopped to think whether I was playing by standing orders, or about the long-term objectives. Triggered, I'd gone off. There was no point in recrimination.

The question was: What now?

'Come on,' she said, breaking up the silence. 'Let's hear your side of the story.'

'We appear to have stirred up some trouble,' I said tiredly. 'To put the worst possible interpretation on things, we seem to have started a revolution. Not by any fault of our own, but simply by arriving at the wrong time. The colony is administered from the capital – Hope Landing – but really controlled by a small aristocracy of the mind who live on an island offshore from the town we just ran away from. Jason took Nathan to see the puppet masters, and one of the puppets hit me over the head. The logic seems to be that if we can be persuaded to deal with the administrators, the Planners' monopoly of Earthly knowledge won't be worth a damn – and their power will automatically be broken. Ergo, the planners are mad keen to keep us to themselves, and the rebels are just as keen to co-opt us. The result is that all the hostility which would have stayed pretty much concealed has suddenly flared up. And here we are, with wasps flying all around. Not pleasant.

'By all the rules, it's the Planners we should be dealing with. They are the actual masters and it's not up to us to question that. The only trouble is that it occurs to me that while the rebels have a very keen and real interest in using us, the Planners might just settle for quietly removing us from the scene with cut throats. The whole situation is rather more complex than that, because both sides are worried about what recontact may mean to them in the future, but with things as uncertain as they are my natural pessimism assures me that there's a very real danger of some-one opting for the simple answer . . . which is murder.'

'And you still think we were wrong to run?'

'I don't know,' I told her. It's all very well for the UN to tell us that we're expendable and lay down rules according to that assumption. I don't feel very expendable, myself. So maybe we should try looking after ourselves. On the other hand, if we'd been able to keep the lid on and everything going smoothly, we might never have got in such a nasty set of circumstances. But here we are, so . . .'

I didn't bother to finish it, and she didn't bother to help me out. Silence fell, for a full minute or more, while we thought about the implications of that 'so . . .'

'It's bloody cold,' she commented finally.

'We've no food,' I said. 'No weapons. No friends. No plans. And on top of that, as you so aptly put it, it's bloody cold. One can't help but feel that the gods are against us.'

'The gods are always against you,' she said philosophi-cally. 'But sometimes you can cheat them.'

Which was a shrewd enough observation. Except that in order to cheat you have to have a chance to stack the deck . . . or to secrete a card in your sleeve. So far, it seemed, there wasn't one of us who'd had a chance to do anything remotely clever.

Perhaps it was time to start.

'It seems to me,' I said, 'that we have two basic choices. Either we go back to the ship and see what can be done there, or we go to the island, and see if we can recruit Nathan to our independent operation . . . or, just possibly, let him recruit us back into his.'

'I don't fancy our chances of getting near that ship,' she said.

'I don't much fancy our chances of contacting Nathan, either,' I admitted. 'It looks like long odds both ways. But we have to opt for one or another.'

'If you were in their place,' she mused, 'which one would you expect us to try?'

'The ship,' I said confidently.

'They'll be ready for us there,' she said.

'But they might not expect us to try to get to Nathan.'

'So . . .'

'How are you with ships?' I asked, in a noticeably lighter tone. 'The kind that float on water.'

'I can row,' she offered.

'So can I.'

We let it rest for a moment while we thought it over. The more I thought the less like a rational plan of action it seemed. Finding Nathan might be like locating the proverbial needle in a haystack. And even the simple business of getting to the island in order to start looking might be far from easy. But the alternative didn't seem to bear much thinking about either. At the ship, they'd be alert. And we already knew that *they* were prepared to play rough. It would be good to spring Mariel . . . but we had no guarantee that she'd still be there. For all we knew she might be on the island herself by now.

It had to be the devil or the deep blue sea, and I always figured that in such a situation you had a better chance with the deep blue sea. . . .

'The island is the real heart of affairs,' I said. 'That's where we want to be, if things take a new turn. You never know – the plot could get sicker yet.'

'OK,' she said. 'I'm with you.'

'But let's take it easy,' I said. 'We have to be careful. The long-term objective is to convince these people that we came to help them, not to pave the way for a takeover bid or to start meddling with their attempts at historical navigation. We have to persuade them to listen to us – and accept that dealing with us won't mean a new wave of colonists with their own ideas and their own know-how.'

'That's not going to be easy,' she said. 'Bearing in mind that it could be exactly what recontact *will* mean.'

There had, of course, been no mention in the prospectus for the operation that *we*'d been shown of any such scheme. But it was natural enough to expect that if Earth wanted to restart the colony project, then exporting people to already established and successful colonies was safer and more justifiable than searching out new possibilities ... especially if the overall success rate was low.

'The UN can't start exporting people to Floria,' I said optimistically. 'It would start a war.'

'But it would be a war that the invaders would win,' she pointed out. 'And they'd win easily. There are no weapons here, remember.'

The attempt to eliminate the possibility of civil war is by no means the best preparation for the repulsion of an invasion. Karen was right: if Earth wanted Floria, then Earth could take Floria, giants or no giants. And when every little thing that might help tip the balance was important in view of the poor state of Kilner's colonies, one perfect world ripe for the plucking might be a weighty factor in the argument.

'Killing us won't help,' I said. 'In the long run, it wouldn't make the slightest difference.'

'Wouldn't it?' She pursued the point remorselessly. 'The *Daedalus* is the only ship in space at this time. Maybe there'll be more going out in the six years we're scheduled to be away, but maybe not. The whole programme hangs in the balance, and could become the victim of any political slogan war. If the Florians destroy *Daedalus* they just might get away with it. Maybe only for fifty years or a hundred ... but maybe forever. Earth's resources keep stretching and stretching, and the propaganda's had them on the brink of extinction for three hundred years and more ... but the time is coming when there just might not *be* the resources for a space programme unless we can somehow co-opt the resources of healthy and active colonies.'

I hesitated, and finally found myself thrown back on the weakest argument of them all – the self-defeating argument.

'The Florians don't know all that,' I stated, without confidence. It was true, of course ... the Florians didn't know all that, and we'd be idiots to tell them. But the implications of that statement were that we were going to be exactly what the Florians suspected us of being: con men trying to win their friendship with false promises. That cap might fit Nathan, but I didn't like it at all. I didn't want to have to wear it.

She wasn't even finished yet.

'And suppose,' she said, 'that the Planners *do* decide to dispose of us. Or have already decided to ... what then? We fight, we run, just as we're doing now. We may die ... but we may also get away with it. And we leave behind ... what?'

I saw what she was getting at. Now that we'd stirred up the wasps' nest it was stirred. We couldn't back out now and say 'Sorry, wrong world.' Recontact had been achieved the moment the *Daedalus* landed, and the consequences of that recontact were going to be felt on Floria one way or another. We had arrived to find a world fighting very hard for permanent peace ... but it wasn't impossible that we might leave one arming for war. Against potential enemies from Earth, or against one another.

Did they ever have a chance, I wondered, of building a new world for themselves? A world that could be different from Earth, a human race with different priorities? Perhaps it was always hopeless while there was any possibility of recontact. Maybe, I thought, it isn't just the people who learn nothing from history who find themselves trapped by it. Perhaps the trap is there whatever you learn.

'It looks,' I muttered, 'like a case of heads you win, tails I lose. For everyone. How the hell are we going to get out of this mess?'

She pointed a finger up into the starry sky. 'Like I said,' she drawled. 'Cheat the bastards.'

CHAPTER NINE

As soon as the daylight came, we began the long march. There was no point in wasting time. We were cold, we were hungry ... and we had a limited time in front of us before we were no longer capable of following *any* plan, however ill-formed and crazy.

The idea – mine – was to double back in a long arc which would take us around Leander to the seashore north of the port. Then under cover of the next night's darkness, we would sneak back into the inhabited area just far enough to find and appropriate a rowboat. We would then row to the island and set about trying to locate Nathan or learn whatever there was to be learned by careful eavesdropping. We had no cards up our sleeves ... our final recourse was simply surrender.

Laboriously, we climbed the long slope at whose foot we had hid out for the night. We were hoping that at the top we might find a vantage point from which we could see the whole extent of the territory we had to cross, and thus identify an easy route across it.

I didn't expect that there would be any organised pursuit or search. It hardly seemed worth it, from Jason's point of view or Vulgan's. There was nothing we could do out here ... we didn't even have enough local knowledge to live off the land for a week. Sooner or later we'd have to come to them, and the only question so far as they were concerned was which one of them would be afforded the dubious privilege of grabbing us. In the meantime, they would be *very* busy ... the conflict had been joined and the sides would have to be drawn up.

From a crag atop the ridge – far above the wrinkled landscape we had traversed during our flight from the station – we could see the buildings of Leander and the harbour. We could also see the island – an irregular lump of rock looking, in profile, somewhat akin to a Poisson curve, with a tall building making up the tip of the modal point. It was some way to the north of the point at which the sun had risen from the sea, but it was still only a silhouette against the brightly lit sky and sea.

There was a spur of land projecting into the sea north of the town, pointing like a thick finger at the island. This spur formed the northern bank of a river whose estuary was so close to Leander harbour that it must have been a good deal easier for ships to leave than to arrive. The harbour traffic must creep in from the south and then move to the north, where the current of the river would carry it out to sea through a relatively weed-clear channel.

From where we stood we could inspect the country strung out between the ridge and the coast almost as if it were a gigantic map. It was hard to follow such minor colonial innovations as the dirt roads and the railroad because the folds of the territory and its forests hid large stretches from view, cutting them into small sections and destroying the visual impression of sequence. Except for the jungle of grey slate roofs that was Leander the humans, from this elevation, seemed to have made very little impact on the land. But this was not farming land. To the south – which was hidden from us by the hills – we would have seen a different kind of picture, with square divisions chopping up the territory into a multitude of regular segments, each one the symbol of human domination.

Away to the north, beyond the river, there was a large flat area of mottled green and silver, with occasional streaks of brown mud. This I judged to be salt marsh – not a tidal marsh but a static one, with land slowly being whittled away by the corrosive flow of the river and its attendant streams, being reclaimed inch by inch into the ocean.

Scattered on the north bank of the river there were a number of huts, which did not seem to be permanent dwellings but buildings erected for occasional convenience.

I pointed them out to Karen. 'That's where we'll find our boat,' I said. 'We won't have to go into town. That's a base for occasional forays into the salt marsh.'

'Why would they want to go into the salt marsh?' she asked.

'Because it'll be teeming with what passes for animal life on this world. Pretty repulsive creatures, for the most part, but all good solid protein. The people might find it unpalatable but the pigs won't. It's not enough to make an industry out of, but a few men sallying forth once or twice a month to pick up what they can could certainly make a worthwhile thing out of it.'

'How do we cross the river?'

I pointed almost due north, to a point at which there was a rough wooden bridge, half hidden in a clump of trees. It was only a footbridge, and the path which led to it wasn't very noticeable.

'That's silly,' she said. 'Why would they build a bridge there, in the middle of nowhere? There isn't a house for miles.'

'At a guess,' I said, 'it's the narrowest part of the river. Closer to the town a bridge would be a major engineering challenge, but that's just a few logs spanning the water. Just for the sake of having a bridge available in case they want to go out into the country to the north.'

She was measuring the distance between the river mouth and the island. 'The current will help us,' she said, 'but it's still a fair way to row.'

'The sea's calm,' I pointed out. 'The sea's *always* calm. We can do it easily. No trouble at all … so long as they leave lights in the window to guide us. And why shouldn't they?'

'Fair enough,' she replied.

We began to scramble down the slope on the other side of the ridge. It was almost exactly like the one we'd come up: the rock was firm but badly rutted. The crevices where vegetation grew with the characteristic Florian luxury offered an abundance of hand- and foot-holds, but could not always be trusted. Sometimes the plants would simply tear away from their anchorage in a shower of loose soil. It would have been a dangerous climb had the face been steeper, but we were able to choose a fairly simple way which took time but didn't expose us to any real danger. I tested all my holds carefully, and not until I was almost at the bottom did one give way and spill me over. An apparently firm plant found my total weight too much to bear, and was ripped loose, roots and all, in my left hand. I scraped an elbow painfully in scrabbling for support, but was fortunate enough not to damage an ankle.

When Karen arrived, moments later, to check that I was all right, I had already given up the morbid inspection of minor injuries and was examining the plant thoughtfully.

'This is no time for collecting botanical specimens,' she commented sarcastically, 'and that's no way to go about it.'

'Look at it,' I said.

It had a tough, slender stem, thickened into wood but still elastic. It had many branches and leaves, arranged in the complex but exact and symmetrical geometrical pattern typical of Florian vegetation. The branches bore tiny conical seed-bearing structures, pale yellow in colour, at their extremities. From the tip of the root-net to the crown of the foliage the plant was something under eighteen inches long . . . and yet it was unmistakably a tree.

'So what?' said Karen, having inspected it.

I looked around, and then pointed to a tree which was growing in the deep soil of the valley floor, well away from the shadow of the rock face. I walked over to it. It was some twenty feet high, but otherwise very similar in structure to the plant I held in my hand. My intention was simply to show Karen that my plant was a miniature of the larger one, but as I approached the big one and compared it with the one in my hand I began to realise the extent of the similarity.

It was not simply that they were different representatives of the same species. The small tree was *identical* in all but size to the larger one. It had the same number of branches, and the extent of its development was the same. It had the same number of seed-cones, each one a perfect replica, albeit very tiny, of the ones on the greater tree.

'Well, I'll be damned,' I murmured.

'That's nice,' said Karen, still sarcastic. 'It's a baby one.'

'It's impossible,' I said. 'These things are identical. They must be brother trees – germinated at the same time from similar seeds. Genetically and developmentally identical in all respects but one. But that's just not possible.'

'It seems reasonable enough,' she objected. 'The one you're holding was growing in a little tiny crack with hardly any soil, shielded from the sun for some of the day. *That* thing's got all the sun and soil it could wish for.'

'And so,' I said, 'it's grown to be a nice, healthy giant . . . like everything else on Floria. But what I want to know is how *this* one managed to grow at all. It had the bare minimum requirement for growth ... it could germinate, and begin to grow ... but not like this. It should have started out and then failed. Maybe it could stay alive, as a weedy stem with a couple of branches, but that's not what it's done – it's reproduced the form of the healthy tree *exactly*. It's developed perfectly – on a much smaller scale. It's as if it knew when it started out that it couldn't grow to be big. But that's not the way things work ... growth is genetically programmed. A plant can't just "decide" to stay small. Its development should have been short-circuited ... it should never have grown to be a fully mature individual.'

'But it did,' she pointed out. It was information I didn't need. Despite my specialist's eye, I had only just seen the evidence of the fact that Florian plants and Earthly plants had one more vital difference in their capabilities. I had been assuming too close a similarity. Because a tree is a tree, and grass is grass, anywhere on the colony worlds. ...

I should have been the last person to fall into the obvious trap of taking things for granted, but it's such an easy trap.

'This is it,' I said quietly. 'This is the key to the giantism. But how does it work?'

'I've seen miniature trees on Earth,' said Karen. 'They call them *bonsai* or something similar. It's an ancient Japanese art.'

'That's different,' I told her. 'As you say, it's an art. It requires elaborate care and a certain degree of surgical interference. But here we have a kind of self-regulation. What has happened is that the primary roots have somehow "informed" the developing embryo of the limitations of the environment in which the seed was growing – and because of this the whole developmental process has changed gear, so that instead of getting a stunted, useless plant trying to grown to "normal" size and failing miserably we have a plant which comes to full, healthy maturity despite the conditions of deprivation. That's quite some trick. The plants here are more highly developed than the plants on Earth, in terms of efficiency and organisation of form, but this is something else.'

'It's only a matter of size,' she complained.

'There's no *only* about it,' I corrected her. 'The matter of size is the heart of the problem. I wonder how they work the trick.'

'What about the reports on the original survey?' she asked. 'And the work that was done on the Florian plants brought back to Earth – wasn't there anything in the reports on this?'

I shook my head. 'There wasn't enough work done. People got very touchy about the handling of plants brought back from other worlds ... and rightly so. You don't take risks of that magnitude. Everything had to be done with the strictest quarantine regulations in force. And the question they wanted answers to was really a very narrow one: Could Earthly animals thrive on this particular alien produce? Basically, what they did was feed the stuff to test animals to see if it killed them. It didn't. Answer to question: Yes. All other observations were incidental, with no comprehensive background study to tie them in together. A hell of a way to run a scientific investigation – but everyone knew that the volunteers were taking a big chance anyhow, and you know what committees are. Expenditure, in terms of effort as well as cash, has to be pared to the minimum. You can argue till doomsday about what constitutes a reasonable risk ... and we very probably will. So, in brief, the original work on Floria's life-system was inadequate. In a sense, the colony itself is the main experiment. The whole colony project is just so many experimental runs under slightly different conditions, and it's still to early to register a final decision. Can men survive in alien life-systems, and if so, how? We still don't know ... not really.'

I dropped the miniature tree, and wiped the dirt from my hand. I continued to look at it, still trying to sort it all out in my head. There was light at the end of the tunnel, now. I could make a reasonable guess at the cause of the growth epidemic. The probable answer didn't fill me with joy and happiness.

Karen put her hand on my arm.

'Are you OK?'

'Sure,' I said. 'I'm sorry. We're wasting time. Let's get on.'

She seemed slightly uncertain. I smiled reassuringly. 'It's all right,' I said. 'It's just that for the first time I can smell the rat I'm here to catch.'

CHAPTER TEN

One of the most useful features of the all-purpose clothing which we'd been issued for this expedition was the fact that it was water-repellent. The gaps could all be sealed so that – if and when it became necessary – we could wade through water neck deep and stay dry.

In the salt marsh, it almost came to that.

We had no trouble getting across the bridge unseen by human eyes, but in order to make use of the structure we had been forced to come so far upstream that there were three or four miles of marsh to be traversed before we got to the group of huts. We couldn't walk along the river bank itself, because there were paths running alongside the south bank. We had to go some way north so that the tall reeds and swamp shrubs hid us from any passersby across the river.

It wasn't easy forcing our way through the rushes which grew wherever there was exposed soil – all the tiny islands in the marsh were packed tight with all manner of growths. For the most part, it was easier to wade in the shallows beside the islets, though we couldn't avoid the rushes without swimming.

Progress was slow. I led the way, armed with a long stave I'd broken from a tree and trimmed with the aid of Karen's iron bar, which was flattened at the hooked end and made a fairly serviceable scraper. I used the stave to test the depth of the water we were walking in. The bottom was invariably glutinous with silt and organic debris, and there were worms and aquatic slugs in some profusion feeding there – none of which made the going any easier.

Occasionally, we came across great flat carpets of vegetation which seemed to offer a much easier way, but these were invariably floating rafts of tangled stems, and when we attempted to walk on them we could not persuade them to support our weight for more than a few seconds at a time. They gave the impression that if we were to run lightly over their surface, not pausing at any one point, we could avoid sinking, but the business smacked too much of tightrope-walking. If one of us were to fall into the middle of such a raft, becoming entangled in the mass of knotted fibre, getting out again might be next to impossible.

We stopped, occasionally, on a convenient islet for a rest. Most of the squat trees were decked with creepers and coloured fungoid growths, but it was usually the work of a couple of minutes for Karen to clear a space to sit with a few graceless swings of the crowbar, in whose use she was becoming adept.

While we rested on such occasions I couldn't help taking to 'fishing' with the pole – trying to lift the denizens of the ooze up to the turbid surface where I could study them briefly before they flapped themselves clear and sank again to the mundane business of life. I would have lifted them out to display them, taking a more careful look at their bodily organisation, but they were of such bizarre colour and shape, and their texture so pliably gelatinous that even I didn't like to handle them.

There are, of course, only three basic styles in animal shapes: spherical, radial, and bilateral – and the first of those is generally restricted to the most elementary of organisms. But the majority of the creatures which I managed to haul up for inspection showed scant respect for any kind of symmetry – radial *or* bilateral. Even on Earth, nothing is *exactly* symmetrical, but here on Floria the basic symmetry underlying every growth process – and to which the plants adhered most rigorously – seemed to have been abandoned by most of the animals as they grew larger. They were untidy bundles of flesh, looking rather like parcels which had come apart in the mail and were barely constrained by loose, tangled string. Even the worms had bulbous processes and groups of tentacles, distributed without rhyme or reason along their length. The creatures which were more bulbous to start with — creatures resembling sea cucumbers, starfish, jellyfish or molluscs — elaborated themselves in all kinds of strange ways.

In water, of course, mass means little, and when your specific gravity is very much the same as that of the mud you inhabit it hardly matters what weird form you adopt, but the sheer profusion of it all was what seemed remarkable. It was not that there were incredibly vast numbers of organisms so much as the fact that there seemed to be no two *alike*. Every one I dredged up seemed to be something quite unique. It was an illusion, of course — it was simply that different individuals of the same species might differ considerably in details of form and colouring. On Earth, the human species exhibits two distinct physical forms and a number of minor variations of colour and features but here . . . identity — individual identity — meant so much more. *More,* among the animals . . . but *less* among the plants.

The trees themselves, where we rested, tended to have their animal life: small vermiform creatures not unlike leeches wandered among the branches, as did a profusion of snails (who wore their shells, of course, as a guard against desiccation, not a protection against predators). I looked at these creatures, too, and found their diversity fascinating. Karen, once I had confirmed that the leechlike individuals were not, in fact, leeches, was content to ignore them all. They did not have the same fascination for her.

I was, not unnaturally, tempted to linger whenever we stopped. Over and above the necessity for regular periods of rest I felt that I was under some compulsion to find the basic pattern underlying all this confusion. Occasionally, when the water was very shallow, I could watch the creatures *in situ,* moving slowly through the mud and throwing up tiny eruptions as they dived deeper or 'surfaced'. The creatures I yanked up with my staff were the big, ugly ones, but not all the denizens of the swamp were big and ugly. There were tiny creatures: spiral worms, hydralike creatures, and even ciliates and amoeboid forms comfortably visible to the naked eye. If I cupped my hands and dredged the mud in the shallows I could net thirty or forty tiny creatures which flipped around on my palms as the water drained away through my fingers. They reminded me strongly of the rich profusion of the microscopic protozoa inhabiting ponds and sea-shallows on Earth ... except that these were on a larger scale. No doubt there were microscopic forms *as well*, to complete the spectrum. Except, or course, that the spectrum was not 'complete' in the same way that Earth's spectrum of motile creatures was. For after all these creatures of jellylike flesh were only half-animals, living on decaying organic matter. Only a very tiny fraction of them could eat healthy plant tissue, and virtually none could prey upon their brethren.

The fierce competition for organic molecules – the motive force behind the primary differentiation of primitive cells into molecule-makers and molecule-stealers, and thus into plants and animals – had never been fierce *enough* on Floria. The dice had been loaded in favour of the industrious molecule-makers, and the bandit cells which – on Earth – were ancestral to virtually all mobile, free-living organisms had never flourished.

The analogy between the evolutionary ecology of Floria's life-system and the history of the human colony did not escape me. In this life-system the struggle for existence was not a kill-or-be-killed, eat-or-be-eaten affair, but a competition for efficiency, where the healthiest and most competent won out by producing more offspring. The rigid regime of competition here was found among the plants, which competed for space and light, and all failures were stillborn: seeds which failed to germinate rather than organisms which grew halfway to maturity and then were destroyed. On Floria, evolution was not so cruel. And the Planners wanted to build a society in which cruelty was banished from human relationships.

Was it possible? Was it possible, in *either* case? There was one piece, I knew, still missing from the evolutionary puzzle: the one fundamental thing which was responsible for the difference between Floria's biosphere and Earth's. I knew what kind of piece it was, but I hadn't quite found it yet . . .

Evolution, on Floria, had a kind of built-in indolence. A sloppiness. Animal evolution, that is. The plants were refined, precisely formed, efficient. But the animals got along any old how. They grew large, ugly. They were leisurely in their conduct, content to live on sludge. Soft flesh and idle habits. Why. . .?

In a sense, I thought, Floria is a kind of Paradise. The *pressure* on living organisms is not the same. And because it's a Paradise, it's ugly. The animals are wonderful, but repulsive. Because there's a correlation between beauty and efficiency. A big cat is beautiful because it's been fashioned by evolution to a particular purpose. It is designed to chase and kill. And by the same token, the antelope is beautiful because it's designed to run and escape. The whole process is circular – the faster and more graceful the predator becomes, the faster and more graceful the prey. But not here. Not on Floria. No grace, no speed. Just giants.

The human colony on Floria was going the way of all Florian flesh. Slowly and casually (how else?) the humans were being sucked into participation in the Florian way of doing things.

Today, giants . . . tomorrow . . .

'My God,' said Karen, with feeling, 'this is a *horrible* place!'

A great flattened worm with a ragged fringe had convulsively coiled itself around her leg. It wanted to get away just as much as she wanted to get it loose, but as she stabbed at it with an iron bar it was at the mercy of its own reflexes. It coiled and writhed, and could not get free. I tried to stop her stabbing with the crowbar, but before I had her arms restrained she had slashed the soft flesh to ribbons, and cloudy dark green ichor was bursting from the rubbery flesh. I put my arm down and let the worm wind itself off Karen's leg and on to my wrist, and then let it alone to uncoil itself and go on its way. But as it did so, it was already dying.

'Do you have to start smashing *everything* with that damned thing?' I demanded, with some asperity.

'Hell's bells!' she replied, with more than equal ferocity. 'It's only a goddamn *worm*.'

'It couldn't do you any harm,' I said. 'It's not built to take injuries like that – once ruptured these creatures are as good as dead. They haven't any built-in resilience.'

'What the hell does it *matter?*' she demanded, perhaps more in surprise than in anger.

'The crowbar isn't the answer to everything,' I said soberly. 'Nor is the way you use it. It's for opening boxes ... but ever since you picked it up you've been using it like a battleaxe. That's Earth thinking. It doesn't belong here.'

She looked at me, the surprise dulling into puzzlement.

'You really mean that, don't you?'

'Of course I mean it.'

'You're a fool,' she informed me.

'It may seem rather silly,' I admitted, 'defending the rights of a worm. But I don't think it makes me a fool.'

'It's not just the worm,' she said. 'It's everything. You really believe in all this, don't you? You really have faith.'

'All what?' I said guardedly.

'The mythology of space conquest. The whole bit. Man emerging from the womb of Earth to a mature existence among the stars. Man learning to live on alien worlds, throwing off the shackles of his particular heritage, finding new cosmic perspectives. You believe in the possibility of a new saintly humanity out here in space, free of all the squalor and the viciousness and all the original sins of Earth. You believe in higher destiny ... in the ultimate perfectibility of man ... and you believe there's something tragic in hitting a worm just because it isn't built to cope with being hit.'

The irony in her words was positively scorching. There was only way I could possibly face it.

'Certainly I do,' I told her. 'I believe in all of that. Maybe more. Some of the words are loaded, of course ... but so far as the thoughts underlying them go, I believe in the whole bag. Don't you?'

'You have to be joking,' she said.

'Why? You came out here as part of the same project. You volunteered for space ... accepting a part in all that mythology you're so scornful about. We're both here, on an alien world, wading through an alien swamp in pursuit of the same vague ends . . . what's the difference between us?'

'I'm carrying a battleaxe and you're feeling sorry for a wounded worm.'

I sighed. 'I was afraid you were going to say that.'

She started to look self-satisfied, but she hesitated. She wasn't sure. She didn't know whether she'd won the exchange or not.

'Go on,' I said tiredly. 'There's a long way to go yet.'

We moved off, making the same slow progress. The sun was high in the sky by now, and we were sweating in the humid heat. I still led the way, probing with my stick.

'You know,' I said, without turning my head to face her, 'I have a son who feels exactly the way you do about the conquest of space. He thinks that it's evil. He thinks that we should conquer Earth first, build a Utopia at home before we even think about the stars. But he doesn't understand, you see. He's trapped by his historical perspective. He believes in progress by states . . . levels of technology, if you like. He doesn't realise that all kinds of processes go on simultaneously, that historical time can't be segmented. Even in your life, you have several processes going on simultaneously. All your selves develop together . . . all your personal mythologies grow and develop, each alongside the others . . . That's the way change happens.'

She didn't answer, or indicate that she had even been listening. Perhaps it was all meaningless to her. Perhaps I had already exceeded the limits of her tolerance. But even cynics occasionally take time out to think.

Sometimes.

CHAPTER ELEVEN

We waited in one of the huts until nightfall.

I had hoped that there might be food to be discovered somewhere in the small huddle of buildings, but we were unlucky. Not so much as half a loaf of stale bread did we locate. Just boats, and nets, and miscellaneous tackle. The Florians were a habitually tidy people, not ones to let debris linger and accumulate.

We had a choice of boats. We selected the smallest, believing that it would be the easiest to row. I took the oars first. We launched it into the river and tried to sneak unobtrusively along in the shadow of the north bank. This proved somewhat difficult as the current persistently attempted to drag us out and get a better grip of us. Although it was taking us the right way I found myself fighting it – and losing, thanks to the clumsiness born of inexperience. Within minutes, I realised that the best thing to do was allow the current to have its way. We were far more likely to be discovered because of my inexpert splashing of the oars than through the keen sight of anyone on the bank. A drifting boat occupied by two shadows might not receive much attention anyhow, whereas one obviously occupied by unskilled rowers quite possibly would.

Once beyond the mouth of the river I began assisting the current again, and by the time the river's thrust had abandoned us I had acquired a reasonable rhythm. It never became easy, but I felt that I had mastered the business and was moderately comfortable.

We could see the lights of the town to the south, supported on a raft of liquid light that was their shimmering reflection in the sea. When there was no longer any possibility that we might be noticed, I began to find the view rather beautiful. Karen, who was sitting in the prow of the boat behind me, did not have the opportunity to become lost in rapt contemplation of it all, for it was her business to make sure that I stayed on the right course. Fortunately, the lights of the buildings on the island showed up as brightly as those of the town – individually, in fact, they were probably much brighter, and I guessed that the aristocrats of knowledge made far more use of electricity than the common people. Where wealth is knowledge you get a better class of status symbol.

The weed was not such a hazard as I might have imagined. Close to the shore we moved amid the tips of the frond-forest, and there was no trouble save when I dipped an oar too deeply and contrived to get weed wound around it. Farther out, when we encountered the floating weed, we found the cohesiveness of the rafts rather less than I had imagined. Instead of the tightly knit mats we had found in the marsh – which one could almost run across – we found much less firmly bound aggregations which continually divided and rejoined, and which would part easily to allow the boat through. The weed making up this loose scum was made up of short, thin branching filaments. One could pick up handfuls of it, squeeze the water out, and be left with a pad of compressed tissue feeling something like blotting paper, but which could be pulled apart very easily.

The sea seemed preternaturally full of sound. The sound of the wind – hardly more than a breeze – stirring up small waves which lapped the sides of the boat was negligible, and the muted splash of the oars hitting the water was ordinary enough. But there were other splashing sounds, midway between a clean *plop* and a glutinous gurgle, as vermiform creatures broke the surface and instantly submerged again.

When I exchanged roles with Karen and moved up to the prow of the boat to guide us, I noticed that the water in front of us had a faint luminosity which disappeared as we cut into it and scattered the tiny organisms responsible. I imagined us leaving a black wake in a softly shining sea, but in fact the luminosity was patchy anyhow, and tended to fade as waves rippled though it. Only on nights of utter calm might the sea take on a radiant sheen stretching evenly for hundreds of miles. And even then, with the sea creatures forever blindly active . . .

Nothing is perfect.

One by one, the lights on the island began to go out. But some remained. Most were dim and yellow because the electric bulbs were not directly opposite the rather narrow windows, but one – the one I came to rely on more and more as a beacon – was pearly and clear. It was a window high in the largest building – the one on the peak. It was probably set just beneath the slanting roof. I wondered, idly, how to characterise that building, which was obviously the home of Floria's historical architects. A citadel? A university? A fortress? A library? In a metaphorical sense, it was all of them ... and perhaps in a literal sense it would have to fulfil all roles before its appointed mission was very much older. Times change, even if plans don't.

'How much farther?' asked Karen, not turning around to judge for herself lest she lose the rhythm of the oars.

'Not far,' I replied, letting myself fall into Florian habits.

'*I* don't feel as if I'm getting any nearer,' she said. Her mood could not exactly be described as sunny. It had been a long day and at times we had lacked a certain bonhomie which seems to be essential to co-operative ventures in speculative heroism. In short, we were a bit pissed off with the whole issue, and maybe with one another as well. However, when needs must ...

And needs very clearly did.

'It's easy,' I assured her. 'We're doing fine.'

'It's getting bloody cold again. The trouble with weather is that it has no consistency.'

'Keep hauling on the oars,' I advised. 'Work keeps you warm.'

I leaned over the prow and dabbled my fingers in the water, breaking up the bioluminescent glow a fraction of a second before the boat itself. There was a somewhat louder splash as a worm did its doubling-back flip within inches of the boat. I didn't see the worm but I saw the ripples.

'What *is* that?' she asked.

'Sea monsters,' I replied absently.

She didn't believe me.

'Well,' I said, 'maybe just a little one. But out in the

deeper water ... maybe the warmer water in the tropics ... there are no limits to growth. The deep-living scavengers will be able to grow so big as to make the most gigantic squid ever reported on Earth look like something you'd put in a goldfish bowl. They wouldn't be vicious, of course, but if one of them took sick and drifted up to the surface just as a little rowboat ... or an ironclad liner ... was making its innocent way home ...'

'You're a real joy to sail with, Alex,' she said

'What do you want me to do?' I replied, in a desultory tone. 'Sing sea shanties?'

'You're so beautiful when you're mad,' she countered.

It was on the tip of my tongue to make the obvious reply, but I successfully avoided it. There was, however nothing further to be said. The island was still 'not far' away, but it would still take a lot of rowing to get there. I hoped I wouldn't have to take a second spell at the oars, but Karen wasn't about to let me get away with it. Plaguing the same unpractised muscles a second time made them hurt, and all the blisters rubbed up on my fingers and thumbs burst under the renewed pressure. Even my head began to hurt again.

But we got to the island. In the end.

We were lucky, I suppose, in that we didn't find any jagged rocks or sandbanks, which could have proved a nasty embarrassment, but the seacoast of Floria seemed to be a relatively placid and hazard-free place.

We landed on a narrow 'beach' beneath a shallow sandy cliff. The beach was composed of gravelly pebbles, and when we dragged the boat out of the water we made rather a clatter. The sandiness of the soil face extending into the night above and in front of us was due to the gradual pulverisation of the rock by rain. The sand associated with sea-shores back home is the product of the more careful and extended work of the tides. On Floria, the mills of God were by no means so consistent or so powerful.

The light in the high window was still visible, and we concluded that the cliff was by no means sheer. It still seemed like a good idea, however, to walk along the shore towards the shallower end of the island and then come back up the steady incline of the central plateau. It was the long way around but there wasn't any climbing involved and we still had a lot of the night in hand.

First, though, we searched out a crevice in the cliff – a kind of low-slung shelf rather than a bona fide cave – under which we could conceal the boat. It seemed the appropriate thing to do. ... I'm certain the Scarlet Pimpernel would have done no less.

Walking – even walking in the dark – seemed easy after all that arm-work, but general fatigue induced by our long trek through the marshes soon made it painful. We had not gone far before I discovered a distinct limp caused by the fact that my right leg was trying to do more work than my left and was thus suffering more acutely. Karen seemed to have the same problem.

'Heroism,' I commented, 'is a degrading business.'

But it wasn't a very big island, and the stars were shining more brightly than they had during the previous night. Curiously, I still found my eyes searching the sky for familiar constellations – almost subconsciously – and inducing a sensation of dislocation which was quite different from the sense of strangeness I experienced during the day, when the whole alienness of the world was exposed in the bright sunlight. I suppose an alien Earth is one thing, but an alien universe – heaven with a new mask – is something different, affecting a different part of you. Perhaps, though, it was only the legacy of all those myths that Karen had quoted to me.

The settlement on the island was more ordered in structure and layout than anything I had seen on the mainland. The whole complex measured nearly a half mile lengthways and two-thirds of that sideways. Being built at the higher end of the island it gave the impression of being an ornate architectural crown for an eternal natural formation. The individual buildings had little separate identity, being parts of a corporate whole.

There seemed to be an awful lot of it, when one bore in mind Vulgan's comment about a 'handful' of recruits being taken to the island each year.

The main building itself was at the north-western tip of the isle, and the array of minor buildings was spread out on the shallow slope like a bridal train. The main building was more solid than its cohort, and — unlike virtually all edifices we had previously seen — looked structurally *finished*: unalterable and aloof.

'They didn't throw *that* up in any tearing hurry,' I said.

'It's like a feudal castle,' said Karen.

'That's what we have here,' I observed. 'An intellectual feudalism. It stands to reason that the acme of architectural achievement would be an impregnable temple of knowledge. I bet they keep the books in vaults, and the students wander around like monks in holy orders.'

I was semi-serious. But as I was saying it, something pricked at my mind ... a jarring note. Into such a system, where exactly did a man like Jason fit? He might be knowledgeable, but he was also tough. Who were his counterparts in Earthly history? Cardinal Richelieu? Savonarola? He didn't really fit the picture at all. The thought of Jason made me uneasy.

We made our way slowly and cautiously along the side of the citadel. The ground-floor windows were high, but I suspected that the intention had been to stop people peeping rather than to accommodate seven-foot giants. This place had been built by smaller people, and today's Florian's might be outgrowing its corridors and ceilings ... so much for a structure built to outlast eternity.

Eventually, we found a window with a light that would be accessible if we co-operated. As Karen was a good deal lighter than I, it was I who crouched in order to let her climb on my shoulders.

Kneeling, with her unsteady feet on either side of my head, I waited for her to report. But all she said was, 'Jesus, will you look at that!'

Under the circumstances, it was not a helpful remark.

She jumped backwards and landed on her feet. Because I was taller I didn't need as much lift to let me look in through the window, and so she was able to hoist me up for a few seconds simply by cupping her hands and hauling hard when

I used them as a step. This way, I had only the barest glance of the contents of the room, but it was enough to let me see what had induced her exclamation.

I got only the most fleeting impression of the inanimate contents of the room – its furniture and fittings – because my eyes were drawn immediately to its lone human occupant. She was reclining on a large, shallow couch, her body cradled by cushions and her head supported by cushions. She was reading by the light of an electric bulb. The book was a large volume, ill bound but undoubtedly heavy. It had obviously been produced here on Floria. She supported its weight easily, but the fingers with which she was controlling the pages were clumsy. Her hands were massive, but far more massive in terms of bulk than dimension.

The same thing applied to her body. Its length was difficult for me to estimate but its mass was quite phenomenal. She must have weighed at least three times as much as myself. The flesh ballooned out from her frame, seeming to spill out on the couch like a great fluid mass. Her forearms were thicker than my thighs.

Her face was folded, because the aggregation of the flesh could not be constrained by the structure of the skull. It was discoloured – yellowing in the cheeks and the chin. It was also wrinkled and lined . . . seemingly the wreckage of a face rather than anything real and alive. There were eyes, and a bulbous nose, and lips showing irregular teeth as breath oozed in and out of her mouth, but the whole impression of the visage was monstrous, hardly human at all.

I could not judge her age from what I saw . . . but I could guess. . . .

When I hit the ground again as Karen released me I had not the presence of mind to save myself from falling. But the sound of the tumble was muffled, and must have gone unheard. We moved on a little way, though, before we risked whispering again.

'Did you see it?' hissed Karen unnecessarily. 'Like one of those goddamn jelly things you fished up out of the swamp mud.'

'The similarity had struck me,' I murmured. 'Everything

grows big on Floria . . . it puts entirely new meaning into the phrase "growing old".'

'You think . . .' she began.

I interrupted quickly. 'No, it's not just a matter of getting old. It's a matter of living a sedentary life. The people on the mainland are active – all of them. *Everyone* is involved in labour, in making things. They managed to strike a kind of balance. But here . . . the people who *stay* here, devoting their lives to the conservation and management of the legacy of Earth . . . they *can't* balance it out. They're completely at its mercy. Like the things in the mud, there's no limitation on the ways of their growth . . . except that human bodies aren't geared to put on mass indiscriminately. . . .'

'It's obscene,' she said.

I shook my head slowly, forgetting that it was dark and that the gesture conveyed no meaning. 'It's normal,' I said. 'They've grown accustomed to it. They're martyrs to it. It's their price . . . the price they pay for assuming the burden of imitating God. These people have no problems . . . they say. And they mean it. They've absorbed this into the manner of their living . . . so far. . . .'

'But how much longer?' she asked. 'If it's still getting worse . . .'

And that, of course, was the big question

I didn't attempt to answer it. You can't answer questions like that when you're crouching in the dark and whispering.

'Come on,' I said, instead. 'Let's find the door.'

CHAPTER TWELVE

It wasn't locked.

They weren't expecting burglars. They had built the place like a fortress, to withstand bombardment and siege, but they hadn't bolted the door. Maybe they didn't expect the revolution so soon. Maybe they were in for a big shock before too much water had flowed under the metaphorical bridge.

As the door clicked behind us we paused to accustom our eyes to the light. It seemed as if it had been dark forever. We were standing in a short hallways illuminated by a naked electric bulb set in the wall at the foot of a narrow staircase leading off to the right. I moved forward to peer up the stairs, and saw that the corridor at the top was also lighted.

'Must have money to burn,' I muttered. 'Wasteful.' Again, I supposed, it was a matter of status symbology. Here, if nowhere else on Floria, the clothing of night had been banished.

I glanced briefly along the corridor at the doors farther along, and then began to climb the staircase. Karen came after me, and whispered, 'Where are we going?'

'Exploring,' I replied. 'I'm going to find that room under the roof with the bright light burning. It was still on when we came along the side of the building, though most of the others had been switched off.'

'It might only be another fat lady reading in bed,' she said.

'Not on the fifth floor,' I pointed out. 'People built like that don't climb stairs.'

She shrugged, obviously being unable to supply a reasoned alternative. Actually, from here on in we were playing it strictly by ear. The object of going to look for the light was really a fake, just to help keep up the illusion that we knew what we were doing.

The staircase doubled back at each floor, and from every landing corridors extended away in either direction. Each one extended into darkness, for the lights which burned permanently were apparently intended primarily to light the staircase itself.

The top floor was, as I'd guessed, the fifth. We made our way carefully away from the stairhead, feeling in more imminent danger as we moved between doors behind which were supposedly occupied rooms. It didn't take long to find the one we were searching for, because the door was slightly ajar, allowing a tall, thin beam of light to cut across the deep shadow of the corridor. As we approached, we could hear the sound of voices within.

Tiptoeing so lightly as not to make the slightest sound, we made our approach. I found that there was a sufficient gap at the hinged edge of the door to peep through. I moved to do so, simultaneously extending my hand back to catch Karen and warn her to be still. As I touched her hand I felt her draw the iron bar from her belt. I wanted to tell her to put the damn thing away, but I daren't make a sound – and in any case, once I realised who and what was in the room my mind was on other things.

The *who* was interesting enough. It was Arne Jason in earnest conversation with a young man I hadn't seen before. But the *what* was far more interesting ... because while Jason was leaning over the young man's shoulder, the young man was manipulating the controls of a radio transmitter.

So it was not just a matter of leaving certain technological toys undiscovered, I thought. The Planners had their privileged methods. *This* was how Jason had found out about us ... he may even have picked up our signal from orbit but decided to let it go unacknowledged. And this was how information had travelled so much faster than the express train so that Jason had been on hand at Leander to meet us. Agents of the Planners moved in mysterious ways – ways which were mysterious, at any rate, to the people who were being manipulated.

'Why don't you leave it for tonight?' the young man was saying. 'I'll let you know immediately anything comes in.'

Jason, with the edge of impatience in his voice, said, 'How do you expect me to sleep? The whole mainland might be on the brink of falling in step with Ellerich and Vulgan ... and all we get is silence. What's the point of an information system if they won't *use* it properly?'

'Perhaps you've overestimated the danger,' suggested the other, with more than a touch of temerity.

'I've underestimated nothing,' said Jason scathingly. '*I* know what Vulgan and Ellerich are up to even if the idiots that are supposed to be watching them don't. We have to find out how the loyalties are going to divide, and we have to know tonight, not next week or next year. We've *nothing* on the two Earthmen and I *still* don't know which way the Planners are going to jump despite the stuff I fed them. I should never have brought Parrick here ... I should have dumped him in the sea and blamed Vulgan.'

Perhaps wisely, the young man failed to comment on any of this, but remained intent on his controls. It was obvious that nothing was happening and that his intense concentration was contrived. He undoubtedly wished that Jason had taken up his suggestion and gone somewhere else to worry. Nothing was likely to happen at this time in the morning that would demand instant reaction. Nothing, that is, except something completely crazy like the two missing Earthmen turning up on the doorstep to listen in at the keyhole.

I contemplated the scene within. Jason seemed like a very worried man – and maybe with good reason. But where, I wondered, were the Planners? Why weren't they gathered around a table planning like crazy? Their dynasty was on the brink of its greatest crisis, and where were they? In doubt, apparently, about what to do with Nathan as a consequence of what Jason had 'fed' them. The implications of that word, I mused, might be very significant indeed. Could it be, perhaps, that the Planners *didn't actually know* how critical the situation was? Jason and his agents, it appeared, were the Planners' eyes and ears, arms and legs. If the men at the top of this aristocracy, like the men at the top of most aristocracies, were all old, all fat, all useless, then whose was the hand that *really* pulled the puppet strings here on Floria . . .?

As I watched Jason through the crack, that question suddenly seemed very important.

And then the giant turned, and – without warning – headed for the door. I jumped back reflexively, and there was nearly a nasty accident as Karen and I collided in the dark. Luckily, however, she was lightning fast on the uptake, and she danced back towards the bend in the corridor at top speed.

It was a long way, and had Jason come straight out he might well have seen us as we went for cover. But he didn't come straight out. As he flung the door back he turned to address some parting shot to the man at the controls. By the time he turned into the corridor we were out of sight. He was even obliging enough to turn the other way and walk away from us.

'Right,' whispered Karen, as soon as he was out of range. 'Let's get in there and call the ship.'

'Wait a minute!' I hissed anxiously.

She had already pushed past me, but I grabbed her arm.

'It's all right,' she said, in a voice rather too loud for my comfort, 'I won't hit him hard. I'll use the blunt end.'

I couldn't argue. There are limits to the amount of earnest debate you can engage in when you're crouching in a lighted stairwell hoping against hope to avoid discovery until you can find *something* useful and constructive to do. Calling the ship might serve no particular purpose, but it seemed like a better idea than anything I could come up with on the spur of the moment. I let her go. She went.

I came into the room a couple of paces behind her. The body seemed to hit the floor with a colossal thump, but he never managed to squeeze so much as a yelp of surprise out of his throat. She didn't waste any time going for the controls, but simply threw the crowbar at me in the fond hope that I'd catch it. She flung it, I thought, a little more aggressively than was necessary.

I caught it, and it stung my blistered hands fearfully. I looked down at it helplessly. She'd wielded it two-handed, bringing it down to strike a glancing blow to the back of the young giant's head. The bar had been roughened by rust and the blow had drawn blood from his scalp.

I knelt to assure myself that no real harm had been done. He was well out, and I guessed that she must have hit him just about as hard as she could, trusting on his thick skull to hold up under the treatment. He was still alive, and the bleeding wasn't copious. I remembered the harsh treatment measured out to the back of my own head, and I couldn't muster any genuine remorse. If the game was to be played rough, adopting the role of pacifist might be something of a handicap.

Karen was holding a pair of earphones in her left hand, holding them to the side of her head, while the fingers of her right hand jabbed at the knobs on the set.

'Damn stupid way to design a radio,' she muttered.

I closed the door quickly, and felt a lot safer for it.

She paused, listening hard, and then began drumming her fingers on the console. Every ten seconds or so she reached out to reverse one of the switches.

'Come on, you idle bastards,' she said urgently.

I presumed that the signal she was sending would trigger an alarm of some kind aboard the ship – an alarm sufficient to wake a sleeping crewman.

Then came success.

'Pete?' she said, her voice rising above a whisper now. 'It's Karen.'

She beckoned to me, and I came closer, putting my ear close to the receiver. I heard the tail end of what Pete Rolving was saying: '. . . get hold of a transmitter?'

'It's the one I carry in my pants pocket,' she replied. 'How the hell do you *think* I got hold of a transmitter? It's one of *theirs.*'

'I thought . . .'

'I *know* what you thought. All the time you've been sitting around contemplating your arse you *could* have been eavesdropping on their broadcasts.'

It didn't sound to me like the way a good spaceman should talk to her captain, and I daresay Rolving thought the same, but she didn't stop for complaints.

'Look,' she said. 'I'm with Alex. We've made it to the island which is where the whole mess is being managed . . . or not managed as the case may be. We're pretty sure Nathan's here. I think they got Mariel but I'm not sure where. Do you know *anything*?'

'Conrad and Linda are with me,' said Rolving, not wasting any time. 'Not hurt. They tried to bluster their way in and then decided to use muscle. I don't think it was planned – they just fancied their chances because they were so big and Conrad was so small. We're sealed up tight waiting for them to come knocking. So far, it's as silent as the grave. We're worried ... the very least they could do is start delivering ultimatums so we know where we stand.'

'At present,' I said quickly, '*nobody* knows where we stand.'

'*That*,' said a voice from the door, 'is truer than you know, Mr Alexander.'

I turned, feeling as if something supporting my stomach had just been whipped out from under me.

It was Jason, his hand still on the doorknob.

He looked at me, and at the crowbar in my hand.

'Try me, Mr Alexander,' he invited.

I didn't try him.

'Hello, Pete,' said Karen, speaking in a remarkably level tone. 'We just got caught. Figure out their frequencies and tune in on their messages, will you? We'll call you again, if we can. Or maybe now the secret's blown they'll call you themselves.'

Throughout this speech, Jason didn't move. He just stood in the doorway and waited. Karen switched off the transmitter and laid the earphones down. We waited for the big man to make the next move. He seemed to be in no hurry.

Finally — and surprisingly — he closed the door behind him. He extended his hand, and I passed the crowbar over to him. It all seemed very civilised.

Jason looked at the weapon and peered closely at the small bloodstain. He looked down at the fallen man but made no move to check up on his condition.

'He isn't dead,' I said helpfully.

He looked at me calmly. 'You've done very well, Mr Alexander,' he said. 'Very well indeed. I didn't expect this ... not at all.'

He wasn't being sarcastic, but he wasn't complimenting us on our excellent showing either. I knew that somehow we'd played into his hands.

'Why did you come back?' I asked.

'I heard him fall,' Jason replied. It seemed that the luck which had brought us so far had run out abruptly.

'What are you going to do now?' I demanded aggressively. 'Drop us in the sea and claim Vulgan did it?'

'So you *did* overhear,' he purred. 'You mustn't take what I said too seriously. It was an expression of ... frustration. I never really contemplated killing you. Not *then*.'

'And now?' asked Karen.

He gestured at the man on the floor. 'There are easier ways,' he said. 'After this, you don't have a prayer so far as winning the Planners around to your way of thinking goes. They're going to command you to get off our world and never to come back.'

I was slightly puzzled. 'Is that what you want?' I asked.

'That's what I want,' he confirmed. 'Just that. That's why I didn't acknowledge your signal originally. Afterwards, I realised that you'd land anyway, and that there was no way of concealing your existence. And so ...'

'You thought you'd try to persuade us to leave,' I said. 'You were taking two of us to see the Planners, and in the meantime you tried to hijack the ship. The Planners don't know about that, do they? In fact, the Planners probably don't know very much at all about the way you're running things in their name. I'm surprised you haven't disposed of them altogether. But you need them too much, don't you? You need the knowledge which is the key to their power ... and you need them because it's they who command the loyalty of the most of the men who take your orders – and most of the people in the colony, come to that. While the Planners control the people with ignorance, you control the Planners the same way. Is that it? Is that the way you play the game?'

'You're very astute, Mr Alexander,' was all he said.

'You want us out of the way because we're a big threat to your power,' I said. 'The Planners will probably think the same way. But you're afraid, aren't you, that it won't quite work out? You're not sure the Planners will refuse to have anything to do with us. You're afraid they might make a deal – in fact, you're almost as afraid of the Planners making a deal as you are of Vulgan and *his* friends making a deal ... because it's you, and you *alone*, who is desperate to maintain the *status quo*.'

'I'm glad you have it all worked out,' he said, without any trace of anger or animosity. 'It saves explaining.'

It didn't take any additional brainwork to see what he was getting at. Now *he* wanted to make a deal. It was a three-cornered contest. I'd been right when I'd said that the plot could get sicker yet.

CHAPTER THIRTEEN

Once Jason had decided that he had to negotiate with us – whether he liked it or not – he was prepared to treat us with a degree of civility. He did not, however, work hard to cultivate the illusion that we were or might ever become the best of friends. There was always a note of mockery in his politeness. He still thought that his was the best hand in the whole game.

He took us down to the kitchens and procured some food for us. He didn't exactly cook it with his own hands, but he wasn't averse to fetching and carrying it from the various storage cupboards. He didn't bring in anyone else – I think he wanted his talk with us to remain as private as possible.

I washed my hands at a sink, and he watched with a degree of amusement as I gingerly mopped out the wounds left by the blisters. He seemed to think that it was appropriate in some way that we had suffered somewhat in getting here.

He waited, patiently, while we ate, and then led us to a small sitting-room which was presumably his own. I slumped gratefully into the proffered chair like a bag of bones, drained of all strength and just about all feeling. Karen remained uneasy and unrelaxed. She gave the impression that she was still on edge, still ready to leap into action at the slightest provocation. It was useless.

'I didn't expect you to come here,' said Jason. 'After you refused my invitation, I thought you would go back to your ship.'

'And suppose I had accepted your invitation?' I said. 'Would I have been brought here? Or secreted somewhere, like Mariel?'

'To be quite honest,' he replied, 'I'm not sure. It might have depended on the answers you could provide to certain questions. However, it really doesn't matter now. The situation has changed. Now, we can work together ... because your best interests coincide with mine.'

'I find that difficult to believe.'

'I've heard the arguments which your associate has put to the Planners. I've also heard what the Planners have had to say in reply. They were hostile from the start – you must have realised that by now, and you must know why. You represent a threat to everything that they hold dear. Contact with Earth, to them, means contact with all the mistakes that they think they have avoided here. It isn't that they fear the importation of technological knowledge and methods, you understand ... that's the error that Vulgan has made. What they fear is the importation of certain *ideas*: what they see as mistaken perspectives and corrupt ethics. The Planners are trying to keep violence out of the history of this colony – they feel very strongly about violence. Don't misunderstand me ... they're not trying to eradicate violence altogether, certainly not at a personal level. They recognise the bounds of possibility. But what they *do* want to do – and what they believe that they *can* do, given the chance – is to provide for a word without wars. They want to extend this colony over the whole surface of the globe, make Floria a human world, without the large-scale bloodshed which has ... *haunted*, shall we say? ... the history of *your* world.

'Perhaps you will consider the Planners naïve, Mr Alexander. But you must try to see their point of view. The original colonists left Earth determined to make a *better* world, not simply *another* one. Perhaps that determination has become dilute and meaningless in the colony at large ... but here, in this building, it remains as strong as ever. It has been handed down from mind to mind over the years, with all the attendant passion. The Planners are fanatics.

'You see, then, why they were prejudiced against you

from the start. But they are, it seems, not quite as dedicated to their fanaticism as even I might have expected. For one thing, they recognised – as perhaps their ancestors had realised – that contact with Earth might, in the long run, be inevitable. As long as Earth has ships, we cannot keep them away. . . .

'And so they were prepared to talk to Mr Parrick. Listen to what he had to say. They were prepared to drive as hard a bargain as they could, but they were prepared to listen to anything which would not compromise their basic principle. They want no more colonists here, and no Earthmen polluting the minds of their beloved people. But they were prepared to try to buy that freedom, if there was any way that they could . . . rather than simply refusing point blank to have anything to do with you.

'The extremists among them have argued that *any* contact with Earth is intolerable – a threat to the whole future of the colonists. At the other extreme, some have argued that we have something to gain from limited, controlled contact with Earth. The issue is balanced. The main factor affecting that balance, Mr Alexander, could well be *this*.'

The object which he held up, of course, was Karen's crowbar.

'Injuring one man helped,' Jason went on. 'Injuring a second – and within the Planners' own home – will almost certainly underline the anti-contact arguments powerfully. The Planners will hear you tomorrow, of course, and you'll have a chance to talk your way out of it . . . but somehow I don't really think you can do it. Do I make myself clear?'

'Not exactly,' I said. 'I know where *we* stand . . . but what about you?'

'Mr Alexander,' he said levelly, '*I* rule this world. I say that openly because you know by now. We have no secrets from one another. The Planners are old and fat. Their minds live on under mountains of flesh . . . but they have nothing except the power of thought and knowledge. And that isn't enough. It isn't enough to do what they want to do, to do what they think they *are* doing.

'I stand in the middle, between the ignorant, helpless

colonists and the all-knowing, helpless Planners. I am the body of one side and the brain of the other. Both sides need me ... and because of that need I control *everything*. I'm not talking about ambitions, as Vulgan must have ... I'm talking about the way things are. I rule this colony because the way things are arranged permits no one else to rule.

'When you come here to deal with this colony, you come here to deal with me. Not the Planners, not the farmers, not the Colony Manager.'

'That's not so,' I said. 'We came to deal with the colony as a whole.'

'But I'm the only man who can speak for the colony as a whole,' he countered.

'I don't accept that,' I told him.

'You have no real alternative,' he said coldly. 'That is the fact. But that's not really the point. The point is that the best course for both of us, at this stage, is for you simply to return to your ship and fly away into space. Go back to Earth, or on to other colonies. But if your intentions are peaceful, and you came to help, and you have no intention of landing more colonists here in opposition to our wishes – and these are all statements your associate has made – then there is only one way that you can prevent trouble and violence ... and that is to *go away and stay away*.'

'You can't stave off the inevitable,' said Karen. 'Even the Planners recognise that.'

He turned to look at her. 'I can try,' he said. 'And I can succeed. You forget that we have different points of view. They are interested in the future ... in the whole future history of the colony. When they think about avoiding contact, they think about avoiding contact *forever*. That's impossible ... perhaps. But I'm not interested in forever. I'm interested in ten years, in twenty years. I'm interested in *now*.'

'How old are you?' I asked him.

He smiled. 'Oh, I have twenty years in me yet,' he said. 'I won't turn into a mass of flesh that can't even walk. I'm active, Mr Alexander. I *use* my body. That's ...'

'I know,' I said rudely. 'That's why you run this world and not the Planners.'

He looked at me steadily for half a minute or so. His temper was still under control. 'It seems that you don't want to go away,' he said softly. 'You're very determined to help us in spite of ourselves, aren't you? I don't really understand that ... unless, of course, you have motives which you aren't declaring. But tell me this, Mr Alexander. Exactly what alternative do you think you have? You can't deal with the Planners – and if you ally yourselves with Vulgan and Eller- ich you'll help us straight into strife and make a mockery of all the promises Parrick has made. *Is* that what you intend to do?'

'No,' I told him.

'Then what *do* you have in mind?'

'I think I can make the Planners see reason.'

He began to laugh, to make the proposition look foolish. But he knew that I wasn't playing the fool. It was no laugh- ing matter.

'You can't,' he said.

'Watch me,' I countered. Our stares remained locked together.

'I think you should remember that I have the little girl,' he said finally.

I knew we'd arrive at the last card he had to play. This was the ultimate insurance he had. He still thought he could force a deal, even if we didn't want to make one.

I decided it was time to stop playing hard. I wasn't get- ting anywhere, and I was showing off my dislike rather than using my head. I let myself weaken outwardly.

'I'll think it over,' I said. 'But I need some sleep. I'd also like to talk to Nathan. I'll put your points to him ... but any decision we come to has to be a joint decision, not mine.'

He read into that exactly what he was supposed to read into it: the implication that I was about to change my atti- tude, but wanted to duck responsibility for it. His smile widened.

'Of course,' he said. 'I must find rooms for you both. You're very tired. You can sleep as long as you like. I'll take care of everything ... bringing the Planners up to date, arranging for you to see them. And I'll arrange for you to confer with Mr Parrick beforehand. I'm sure that everything can be settled amicably, if you'll only weigh the arguments carefully.'

'So am I,' I said – and I couldn't help just a slight note of malice creeping back into my voice. 'So am I.'

CHAPTER FOURTEEN

'You're a pair of bloody fools,' said Nathan, with feeling. 'Just what the *hell* do you think you've been playing at?'

'Well,' I said philosophically, 'to put it crudely, it all seemed like a good idea at the time.'

He was angry, and comments like that weren't likely to cool him down any. 'You've undone *everything* I've achieved here. While I've been working my guts out trying to convince these people that our intentions were one hundred per cent pure and noble – and that hasn't been easy in view of the fact that they think I'm the devil's cousin – you've been running loose like a pair of cowboys beating people up.'

'They said the same to David after the Goliath incident,' said Karen, facing me but directing the comment to no place in particular.

'Take it easy, Nathan,' I told him.

'*Easy!* Can't you get it into your head that it *isn't* easy. It's damned difficult. You were *told* to avoid intimidating people at all costs. You were told to co-operate, to capitulate, to provide living proof of the fact that we came with no hostile intentions. You *knew* we were coming into a touchy situation and you've done just about everything in your power to aggravate it. If this mission fails it's down to you two and no one else. You have blown the whole damn thing!'

'I'm glad you think there's still an "if",' I said, trying hard to soothe him now.

'Look,' Karen interrupted. 'You don't understand.'

I put my hand on her arm. 'I think,' I murmured, 'that we'll find he understands perfectly. Jason may think he's being super-clever, but he's only a dilettante ... an amateur Machiavelli. He might have the Planners fooled, but he hasn't fooled Nathan.' I looked at Nathan for confirmation of this.

'He hasn't even got the Planners fooled,' said Nathan, with tired sarcasm. 'They're not idiots either. We had it *all* working. Buckland and I had an understanding ... we could have made a friendly contact with a successful colony. You simply have no idea how much that might mean back on Earth.'

'In political terms,' I said.

'In political terms. *Of course* it's a matter of politics. You know that.'

'Aren't you forgetting something?' I asked.

His gaze was angry enough to suggest that he didn't think he had.

'Problems of co-adaptation,' I said. 'What the ship is equipped to deal with. What we came here for ... apart, of course, from all the political reasons.'

Now the anger began to fade. 'You found out what's causing the unnatural growth?'

I shook my head. 'You don't solve scientific problems like Sherlock Holmes,' I told him. 'It's not enough to look at the clues and then point out the murderer. But I know what kind of problem it is ... and I know how serious it is. But that's exactly what the Planners – and Jason – *don't* know. And what's more important is the fact that they don't know they don't know, if you see what I mean.'

'They think they have a different kind of problem? A trivial one?'

I nodded.

'But the one they have is a killer?'

I nodded again. I still had to wait for a few moments while he changed mental gear.

'All right,' he said. 'Not that it makes any difference to the cowboy act, but go on. Let's hear it.'

Satisfied that we could now talk sensibly I shook my head. 'No time,' I said. 'There are much more important things to discuss. Like what are we going to do about Jason? He has Mariel, and he's not going to be pleased when I go before the Planners and show them six good reasons why they need us here desperately. He wants us *out* – we're upsetting his Machiavellian apple-cart. The peasants are restless and things are getting stirred up at home base as well. He thinks he's losing an empire, and he's going to turn vicious. I want to hear some answers from you about how we're going to look after our ourselves when things blow up.'

'Jason is the Planners' problem, not ours.'

'He has Mariel.'

Nathan went to the window and looked out at the calm, quiet sea. I stood up and followed him. Without turning around, he said, 'We're on Floria, not on Earth. If Jason has committed – or intends to commit – any crimes, then they're Florian crimes, and it's for the Florians to take what action is necessary. Despite what you two seem to think we didn't come here as a party of commandos.'

'It isn't the Florians he'll be issuing ultimatums to,' interposed Karen. 'It's us.'

'I'm sorry,' said Nathan, 'but our hands are tied. Our job is to talk to the Planners. It's up to them to handle Jason.'

'*Why* is it our job to talk to the Planners?' demanded Karen angrily. 'Because they *think* they run this world? Why isn't it our job to deal with Jason, who *really* runs things – or with the people on the mainland, who *want* to run things? Everyone here's a self-elected spokesman for his planet ... only they all want different things from us. So why the Planners? How do we decide that it's *them* we should be talking to and not the others?'

Nathan turned back from the window to confront us both.

'I'll not give either of you a string of diplomatic phrases,' he said. 'I could set out half a dozen moral reasons for not allying ourselves with Ellerich and Vulgan, or with Jason. But the simple fact is that we deal with the Planners because the Planners have what we need. That's all there is to it.'

'And what do we need?' I asked quietly.

'A better world. Floria. A world where the cruel and bloody history of Earth might not be repeated. We need Floria, and we need it the way that the Planners are trying to shape it, not the way that Jason thinks he runs it or the way that Ellerich wants to take it over. We need a Utopian dream, however far from fulfilment. As an advertisement. As a lure. To get space travel going again as a successful political concern.'

'We can't use Floria as a lure,' I said slowly. 'They won't let us bring any more colonists here.'

'We don't have to bring any more colonists here,' he said. 'The example is enough. What can be done here can be done elsewhere. Handled right, one big success could offset a dozen failures. It's the dream that has to be kept alive, you see ... the myth. That's how political games are won. Not with facts, with promises. With good public relations work. If we can build up this world as evidence of the fact that there *are* new lives to be made out here, new worlds to be conquered, we can begin to win the slogan war again. That's why I'm here, you see. It's my job to make certain that the reports we take back tell a very different story from the ones Kilner submitted. That's why we deal with the Planners, no matter how ugly they are or how much you might disagree with the methods they use to achieve their ends.'

'That's great,' I said, with slight distaste. 'But there's just two things wrong. One is that this colony won't be successful in any degree whatsoever unless we can help them beat their growth syndrome. And the second is that they might not be able to handle Jason.'

'I didn't say that it was easy,' said Nathan calmly. 'But if we keep our heads from now on, we have a chance. *If* we keep our heads. As for the first of your thorny points, let's not underestimate you, Alex, and the abilities of your staff. Kilner helped the other colonies ... you can help this one. If a solution is humanly possible, you'll find it, and the Planners will use it. On the second point, well ... let's not underestimate the Planners, either. They know about Jason. And I don't just mean that they have their spies to tell them what he's up to. Their ancestors knew about the inevitability of people like Jason, about the inevitability of the situation which breed people like Jason. People who set out to control history don't usually need lessons in it.'

'While we're not underestimating people . . .' I said. 'How about not underestimating Jason?'

'All right,' he said, 'let's not underestimate Jason. He's a determined man. I don't believe that he's acting very cleverly, but he knows what he wants even if he doesn't quite know how to get it. He might threaten Mariel. He might do something else equally stupid. But the vital thing for us to do is *nothing*. We cannot act like bulls in a china shop.'

'If we hadn't acted as we did,' I said patiently, 'I might never have got here. Jason as good as told me that if I'd surrendered to him at Leander I might have been tucked away somewhere with Mariel – and that's certainly what would have happened to Karen. Giving Jason more hostages would be pointless, and could be downright dangerous . . . because if I hadn't gone on the run and come here under my own steam I might never have got into a position where I could explain to *anyone* exactly how much trouble this colony is in. We're *not* just here on a glorified public re-lations exercise – we're here to try and put some *substance* on that dream you want to sell. We can't simply be content to adopt a totally negative role. Maybe we shouldn't have knocked a man out to get at the radio. Maybe Karen over-reacted at the Leander station. But these things have always got to be decided on the spur of the moment, and sometimes a positive attitude is necessary.'

'Forget it,' said Nathan, sighing heavily. 'It's all in the past. You've had your fling, and maybe no damage has been done. If you *can* make the Planners see it your way, maybe things have worked out right. But *please* . . . from now on, we play it my way. All right?'

'I don't know,' I said stubbornly. 'I'm still scared of Jason.'

And at that moment, the door opened, and in he came. I don't know if he heard what I said or not. He showed no trace of emotion on his face. He simply said, 'The Planners will see you now.'

But as I walked past him, I could see the threat glittering in his eyes.

CHAPTER FIFTEEN

They were seven.

They were distributed haphazardly about the room rather than being grouped in the manner of a court or jury. Such grouping would have been impossible. I had expected to find them all old (old, that is, by the standards of this world) and all in the grip of the uncontrolled, quasi-cancerous tissue-growth. But only three – two women and one man – wore bodies which had run completely out of control. These three reclined on couches equipped with tiny wheels. Each of the three had lost all the powers of self-locomotion save one. They could not crawl, nor lift their heads, but the use of their hands remained. While they kept control of their hands, and could continue to use their senses, they retained some essential humanity. When that was gone ... but they seemed, in any case, to be close enough to death.

Of the others, two were clearly losing the fight. They were both men. Both, I think, could have walked – but no great distance. They sat in conventional chairs rather than accepting in advance the need to become recumbent. The remaining two – one man, one woman – were still robust and healthy. The woman, by my estimate, was in her early thirties. The man was the youngest of them all, perhaps no more than twenty-five.

Nathan had already tried to warn me in advance as to which might be sympathetic and which set hard against us. Those he thought he could count on were Edward Buckland – one of the middle-aged men – and Ewan Rondo, the youngest of the seven. The most powerful opposition came from one of the women – Ruth Alcor – and the younger woman would probably back her. The third woman, however, whose name was Viana Calmont, was probably the most influential voice within the group, and she had given no indication at all – so far as Nathan had been able to detect – of where she stood.

We were not offered seats, but left to stand. Jason waited behind us, beside the door. There were some preliminaries. Nathan introduced us by name, but the Planners did not introduce themselves. I was hoping that I would be allowed to make a simple statement, but the Planners wanted things done their way. The youngest man – Rondo – was, apparently as a matter of form, their question-master, and there was something of the attitude of prosecuting counsel in the way he began. Nathan had said that this one was sympathetic, but I guessed that that was in his personal capacity. It seemed to be his duty now to play devil's advocate.

'You're a scientist?' he asked. 'And you came here in order to give us advice, and perhaps assistance, with any problems which fall within your intellectual province?'

'Yes,' I said, knowing there was more to come.

'You do not seem to have conducted yourself like a scientist.'

'That depends on your expectations,' I replied. 'Scientists on Earth don't function in quite the same way as scientists here.' As I said this, my eyes ran over the whole group. 'You practice science in a covert manner. It is the business of an elite. In being kept secret, it has become sacred.'

'You don't approve?' probed Rondo.

'I don't know,' I said honestly. 'But that doesn't matter.'

'You realise that your presence here represents a threat to our aims? You know that your arrival has precipitated a crisis, and that your actions have helped compound that crisis?'

'We have already agreed,' said Nathan, interrupting smoothly, 'that the crisis was inevitable. It is the product of history, and our arrival has done no more than reveal it

132

prematurely. Our actions have made no significant difference.'

'We are talking not so much about a political crisis as a crisis of values,' said Rondo. 'Rebellion against our rule – a rule which is purely theoretical, as we have no legal power – is a product of the social circumstances of the colony. But that rebellion is really immaterial. It hardly matters who is in nominal control of everyday events. It is merely a matter of labelling. What does matter, however, is the prospect of a rebellion against the *values* we have tried to inculcate and maintain in this colony. And your actions – the very assumption under which you act – represent a threat to those values. When challenged, you react violently. You invade our home, secretly, and import violence with you. This is intolerable.'

'We have been violently used ourselves,' I said. I was about to go into detail, but I was conscious of Jason at my shoulder. It was not the time for accusations. It was better to wait ... there was another way.

'This is the whole trouble,' said Rondo. 'You arrive, and violence flares up. With you, violence breeds violence, and the whole situation becomes aggravated, inflamed. That is what we want to avoid at all costs. It is not violence per se which we are trying to eradicate from this culture, but the syndrome by which violence breeds *more* violence, and quarrels become wars. Our aim is to isolate acts of violence from the inflammatory consequences which are inevitable in your way of thinking.'

The one thing that could not be said was: *That's impossible*. That was exactly what they were trying to fight with all the means at their disposal – the acceptance of what they considered to be our way of thinking as natural, rational, and inalterable.

I remained silent, waiting.

The crucial question came.

'Can you offer us any reason why, in view of the danger implicit in your presence here, we should tolerate you?'

'Because you need us,' I said. 'You need us far more than you fear us.'

I heard the quick intake of breath behind me, and it made the hairs on the back of my neck prickle.

'Why?' demanded Rondo, his voice like the lash of a whip.

'You fear us,' I said, 'because we may corrupt you. But if we can do that – if our mere presence here is enough to send all your generations of cunning, considered planning to perdition – then what do you really have as a result of your generations of work? What have you really achieved, if what you have can be sustained only in artificial conditions? Violence is already here, as you know ... and the men who would use it to breed more violence, the men who would exploit violence for their own ends ... they're here, too. The products, I think you said, of history. Perhaps our presence will help them ... except that we are already committed to helping *you*.

'And you need that help. You need it most of all because you do not know how desperately you need it. If I were to say now that this colony faces a danger of extinction within two or three generations, you would not believe me. Perhaps you would be right. I don't know enough, at present, to say any such thing. But I will say this. You have no concept of the nature of the force which has you in its grip. You do not know the extent or the nature of your danger, because you are too close to it. You have not the objectivity to know what is happening to you.

'Perhaps, somewhere, locked in the vaults where you keep your closely guarded supply of human knowledge – knowledge two centuries out of date by Earthly standards – you have the information which would have allowed you to know what is happening to you. But where is the man with that knowledge in his head? Where is the man who uses that knowledge in his everyday work and his everyday thinking? He is not here, because so far as you are concerned that knowledge is for *use*, and for use *only*, in practical terms. You deal in the knowledge which is necessary in order to make and build things ... and in the knowledge which has to be concealed lest certain other things be made and built. Because you have no theoretical scientists, but only applied scientists, you have no one with the broad perspectives necessary to see past your own limited objectives. You have no one, except us.

'And even if you had a man, or men, with a mind educated in such a way that he was capable of perceiving what is desperately wrong here, what could he do about it? You are, I have no doubt, making great strides in medical science and medical technology. But I have no doubt, also, that the science of genetic engineering is one of those areas of knowledge which you have decided – on the basis of good historical evidence – should be left untouched. It is too dangerous, too amenable to misuse. What were its consequences on Earth? Plagues, bacteriological warfare, tragic accidents in ecological management. There were successes too, of course, but history is an interpretative art . . . and it is always easier to explain disasters.

'There is, I believe, no way that you can cope with the disaster which you face, a disaster which already has you in its grip, without our aid. Aid which only Earth can provide.

'It is not a matter of tolerating our presence here – it is a matter of welcoming it and making use of it. I cannot say that if you command us to leave you will all die, or even that your grandiose schemes will be doomed to failure. I only assure you that we are the only ones who can find out how much danger there is . . . and you cannot afford not to know.'

I paused, and looked around at the pairs of eyes that were watching me. They were hostile: each and every one. It wasn't surprising. I was attacking the very roots of all their most precious dreams. Nathan, no doubt, had walked carefully in the garden of their hopes and beliefs, determined not to step on any cherished blossom. He had won such support as he had gained with flattery and promises and sweet words. But I was no diplomat.

Behind me, I heard the door open and close. Without turning around, I knew that Jason had left the room. He didn't know what the outcome of the argument would be, but he already knew enough. He had failed to win us or to make use of us. He felt that all his ambitions were under threat. He had gone to do something about it. While I paused, I wondered what.

But there was no time. . . .

'Tell us, please,' said Rondo coldly, 'exactly what danger you imagine faces us.'

'The flesh on your bones,' I said bluntly. 'And the bones themselves.' He made as if to interrupt, but I held up my hand. 'Oh, yes,' I went on, 'you're aware of the problem. You're seriously concerned about it. But what you don't realise is the full range of its implications.

'When the average height and weight of the colonists began to increase, your forefathers probably thought of it as a good, healthy sign . . . Earthmen growing big and strong in their new world. At first it seemed good, and later, it seemed normal. The change has been gradual, uniform . . . almost imperceptible in a population of ignorant people. *You* knew . . . when the unfortunate corollaries of growth began to appear you became concerned. But only you. And even you fell prey to the same trap. It *seemed* to be normal, to be part of your way of life. In your minds, you knew that you were different from Earthmen and becoming more so. But knowing something intellectually isn't enough of a stimulus. You accepted its consequences, because they were consequences which affect you all, and you have an insular perspective.

'And there's another factor, too: the belief that the man who is obese, or, indeed, loses control over his body in any way at all, is personally responsible. When a man is injured, or invaded by parasites, that is sickness – to be treated. But when a man grows fat, there is the legacy of self-indulgence, a lack of self-discipline – not sickness so much as failure. There is a certain contempt which people feel for other men who become fat and ugly . . . and there is a similar contempt which such men feel for themselves. You *know* – intellectually – that obesity may result from genetic or glandular disorders, but again it is what you *feel* that is preventing you from searching out the whole truth.

'I am sure you have searched for the glandular disorders. I am sure that you have tried to identify, somewhere in the range of foods you use, some chemical compound which is causing your bodies to put on weight unnaturally. Perhaps you have searched for a virus or for an anomaly in the tissue involved. You have tried to see it as a disease, as a cancer. And you have failed. But this only reinforces the feeling that you have that you yourselves are responsible ... that you lack control over your bodies because of some inner inadequacy.'

They were looking at me as if I were mouthing obscenities. I could see hatred in more than one pair of eyes. But I had already cut away all the clothes of convention, the rituals of unmentionability. They were listening. They were hanging on to my every word.

'I don't know how old you are,' I said. 'I don't know how long you expect to live. All the indicators by which I'd try to guess are confused, and even the terms in which I'd have to measure are different. Floria's year is not the same as Earth's year. But I believe that you're dying too soon ... that you have barely as long a maturity as you have a youth, and that your bodies begin to betray you all too early in life. I think that if I were a Florian I would now be barely able to walk. I would be eternally hungry and eternally putting on excess weight by the pound. My life would be almost over. As things are, however, I am perhaps halfway through my life. I have as many years left to me as I have already used. In ten years, in thirty years, I'll still be active in body and in mind. Frail, perhaps, and slow ... but active, still able to *use* my body.'

All this was merely hitting them where it hurt. I wanted to be *sure* of them. I wanted them frightened. I wanted them committed not just to making deals with us, but protecting us as the richest resource on the planet. I wished only that Jason were still here to listen, because I thought I could have panicked even him.

'What you must realise now is that you are still Earthmen trying to live on an alien world. You have deliberately forgotten that fact, tried to bury it. *This* is your Mother World, your only world, the world with which you identify, the world whose substance is the substance of your flesh ... but it is still an alien world, and may always be so. You think you have adapted, but adaptation is something which can take seventy generations rather than seven, and may take forever. As you adapt, the world adapts: and you grow apart as well as together.

137

'You are all being poisoned, by a poison so slow that it takes generations to take effect, and so subtle that you cannot detect it. We can detect it, because we have the resources.'

'All this is very inventive.' The speaker now was one of the older men, not Rondo – the formalities had been abandoned now. 'But it is only rhetoric. You will have to tell us more about this poison you have invented.'

'I will,' I told him. I went on, 'The most puzzling aspect of the giantism which affects you all is its uniformity. This was what troubled me most when I first arrived here. Had it been caused by an individual agent – a hormonal mimic fortuitously manufactured by an alien plant or group of plants – then certain members of your population would have suffered far more than others, and you would have had no trouble identifying the cause. But the fact that *all* of you seemed to have been affected to the same degree suggested that it was something universal – not only in the alien life-system, but in the crops you had yourselves imported. It was several times pointed out to us that on Floria, *everything* grows big. Men, pigs, pigeons, potatoes, even ears of corn.

'I didn't immediately see how that could be, until I'd had a chance to look at things more closely. The *important* fact, and the key to the whole thing, was something I already knew – but only in my mind. It wasn't until I came here, and got out into the wilderness, that I began to see and feel the implications of that fact.

'The balance of nature here is a very different balance from that found on Earth. All the secondary consumers on this world consume dead and decayed matter – the soil is exceptionally rich in organic compounds, the legacy of previous generations of plants. The plants here are superefficient. They fix solar energy quickly, grow quickly – and die quickly. The *turnover* in the energy budget is remarkably high. I was inclined to think that the fact that *real* animals – consumers of living flesh – had never evolved here was because there were no *incentives*. It was too easy to live on decayed flesh, because there was always plenty of it about.

'But that explanation, you see, isn't competent. Where there are opportunities for a new way of life, natural selection will inevitably discover them ... provided that natural selection has a chance to work.

'On Floria, it hasn't. This is partly due to the fact that there are so few regimes of change ... the lack of tides is important here. But it's also due to the fact that there is a factor here channelling change, preventing change along certain lines by permitting it along others.

'Natural selection is so important on Earth because minor changes in genetic structure mean big changes in physical form. Organisms in Earth's life-system have very little innate plasticity. I'm using the word *plasticity* here in a special sense which it assumes within genetic theory: it means the range of different options open to different organisms with identical genes. It's sometimes important in plants when genetically identical seeds grow in very different environments: from one seed you might get a tall plant with abundant leaves, whereas from another you might get a small one with aberrant leaves – these differences can be forced by different limiting factors in the soil. The growth of an embryo is not *entirely* controlled by genes, but also by factors prevailing in the environment where it develops. Now, on Earth only plants have a very considerable degree of plasticity – and by careful management of their growth and judicious interference one can turn out miniature trees or giant fruits. Animals, by and large, have less plasticity ... and among the higher animals, whose embryos grow in carefully regulated conditions within the womb, there is virtually no *natural* plasticity at all. Growth can be stunted by malnutrition, but that's not really the same thing. Muscles can be destroyed and limbs permanently bent by consistent physical interference, but again, that's in no way natural.

'Here on Floria, things are different. *Especially* with respect to tissue growth. I've seen trees which were twins genetically but as far apart on the spectrum of size as one could imagine. I've seen marsh creatures obviously belonging to the same species with a host of small, idiosyncratic differences almost all involving excessive tissue growth locally or generally. Here, all life-forms are individually plastic to a large extent; and where genetic changes make far less difference to the options of a growing organism natural selection is far, far less effective. The animals of Floria, feeders on the dead, have not evolved because they are so *individually* adaptable that new species hardly ever arise.

'The reason why such plasticity is universal has to be that the system of genetic regulation characteristic of this life-system – The way that the expression of the genes is controlled and regulated, not only during embryo-growth but also during functional life – differs somewhat from the system by which the genes in Earth's life-system are regulated. The poison that you, and every other species you have brought to Floria, are picking up here is something rather more basic than a hormonal mimic: it's a compound which interferes with the regulation of genetic programming, with the way the genetic code is read in building and maintaining organisms. Obviously, this regulator compound is not as effective in Earth species as it is in Florian ones. But at this level, compounds are selected for *function*– and just as the photosynthetic agent which makes your grass green is functionally similar to chlorophyll, so this compound is capable of functioning to some degree in Earth-type genetic systems.

'As to where you're picking up the poison *from*, the answer is everywhere. You see, it's in the soil. It's part of the decayed plant-matter which is the staple diet of all organisms on Floria that don't make their own molecules. It's taken up by the imported crops, and it affects them. When your animals are fed on alien food, and even when they're fed on Earth food, they are affected by it, too. And the same applies to you. Whatever grows in Florian soil, or feeds on the produce of Florian soil, picks up this poison.

'Within the Florian life-system, of course, this compound is useful. It is, in fact, central to the whole Florian way of life, in the broadest possible sense of the phrase. In humans, too, it *can* have useful effects. If its effects could be restricted, perhaps it might not be reckoned as a poison at all. But human bodies, you see, were designed by natural selection on the assumption that plasticity was virtually non-existent.

Human genes aren't organised to cope with plasticity. In the developing embryo, the regulated conditions of the womb restrict the influence of the rogue factor to a matter of size: a fairly slight influence, within the spectrum of human practicality. But in the mature organism, which isn't built to last forever, the influence of the rogue factor increases with time – and eventually, the body runs wild. The careful limitations on the behaviour and control of tissues are eroded. You all fall victims to a kind of slow, generalised cancer.

'That is what is happening to you. It has to be brought under control. You have to find a way of coping with this poison; and since you can't avoid it you must find a way of opposing its action. It should be possible ... once we have isolated the compound in the *Daedalus* laboratory and studied its action. All complex biological compounds have weaknesses. We not only have the means to find out what those weaknesses are, and build biological counteragents in the laboratory, but through genetic engineering we can alter plants or micro-organisms in order to make them produce the counteragent for us. We can design a life-form to do the job, to substitute for the laboratory. That's what we're here to do for you, if you'll let us.

'You must not cut yourselves off from Earth,' I concluded, in a voice so soft as to be almost a stage whisper. 'Because, no matter how much you despise all that Earth stands for in your mythology, you remain men of Earth ... and you cannot become men of Floria in the ultimate sense of the word unless you accept all the help that Earth can possibly offer.'

CHAPTER SIXTEEN

They wanted to discuss it. There wasn't really anything to discuss, and we all knew it, but they didn't like the way I'd rammed it down their throats and they were determined to make some kind of show. Karen, Nathan, and I returned to Nathan's room like the accused awaiting the verdict of the jury.

I found, when we got there, that I was trembling. I had to sit down and grip the arms of the chair to hold myself steady.

'When did you work that out?' asked Karen. She sounded a little sour, as if she felt that she might have been let in on the secret earlier. She thought it had all come to me in a flash of divine inspiration when the miniature tree came away in my hand, or when I was fishing in the salt marsh.

'I don't know,' I told her truthfully. 'The pieces just fell into place. Slowly. I wasn't sure when I started exactly what I was going to say. I hoped only that I could make some sense of it. It isn't as simple as that, not really. But I had to make it clear.'

'Are you sure it's right?' demanded Nathan.

'You don't solve scientific problems like Sherlock Holmes,' I told him, for the second time. 'I wish you did. But it's the right way to look at the problem ... and before you ask, I can't guarantee results. All I can say is that if the answer's accessible, we'll find it. Given the chance.'

'You'll get your chance,' he said. 'There can't be much doubt about that.'

'What about *your* chance?' I said. 'Your successful world doesn't look quite as good anymore, does it? There really isn't so much difference between Floria and the other colonies, is there?'

'There's enough,' he assured me.

'What you mean,' I said, 'is that if you write your reports cleverly enough, playing up the right aspects and glossing over the embarrassing ones, you can make this *seem* a very different proposition.'

'You disapprove?' he said. 'But this is all in the service of the dream you hold so dear. Isn't this what you want? The rebuilding of the myth, the reinstitution of the space programme, the union of Earth and colonies ... surely you believe that what I'm trying to achieve is for the good of mankind?'

His voice was mocking, and I was surprised by the sudden aggressiveness. It made me angry. I couldn't make out for a moment or two what I'd done to annoy him, to justify the attack. Then I realised that it might not be anger, but a mixture of contempt and envy. I'd upstaged him before the Planners – and I'd done it with a sincerity, a sense of purpose, which he didn't feel. He was doing a job – playing a game – and he believed only in the game. *Ars gratia Artis.* He looked upon this whole mission as an exercise in manipulation: manipulation of the people with whom we came to deal, manipulation of the great host of committees back home who would have the job of deciding what to do on the basis of our reports. In a way, he was like Arne Jason, the man in the middle, rejoicing in the unique privilege of his situation. History was cupped in the palms of his hands ... but the power to exert his own influence upon it meant far more to him than any sense of purpose, any sense of responsibility. I realized now what Karen had implied when she had told me, back in the village, that not everyone shared my outlook.

'I disapprove,' I confirmed dully.

'You have to be realistic,' he said, his voice becoming normal again after the brief moment of nakedness. 'Don't you?' This addition was aimed at Karen.

'Maybe,' she said, with a marked lack of certainty.

In the silence that followed, the tension which had flared slowly ebbed away. It was a good time to change the subject.

'What's Jason's next move?' I wondered aloud. 'He didn't stay to hear the end of what I had to say. As soon as he knew I wasn't co-operating he was off. Where to?'

'He has only two choices,' said Nathan, who seemed ready

enough to talk about something else and heal the breach, superficially. 'Either he stays with the Planners ... or he changes sides.'

'And?' I prompted.

Nathan shrugged. 'In his present mood, I think he'll change sides. I suspect he already has. It's the wrong decision, of course. But he's tried to play the game his own way, to force things into his predetermined pattern. They wouldn't go. He lost ... and now he's angry. He won't be content to do the simple thing, which is to patch things up, sit back and wait, keeping hold of what he already has. He'll feel a compulsion to act – to *react* against the failure of his naïve little schemes. He needs to hit out, to show off the fact that he really *is* the kingpin and that fate can't treat him thus and get away with it. At least, that's how I read the situation.'

It sounded all too terribly plausible. Jason, his temper flaring, would go to Ellerich and Vulgan. If he couldn't run things from the island in the way he thought he could ... then he would try to run them from the mainland, at the head of the rebellion.

He would hit out. ...

And he still had Mariel. And no one seemed to be doing a damned thing about it. Sit and wait, never act. Talk and think. It was Nathan's way, and it was the Planners' way. But to the Planners – and perhaps to Nathan as well – Mariel was something remote, just another piece on the board, to be moved or taken as the game demanded.

I got up from the chair quickly. I moved towards the door, saying, 'Come on, Karen.'

'Where do you think you're going?' said Nathan, moving to try to block my path.

'To the radio,' I said. 'We have to call the ship, to find out what's going on. Even if Jason isn't handing out any ultimatums yet, Rolving is supposed to be monitoring communications on the mainland. Maybe he can tell us what's happening.'

Nathan hesitated, then nodded.

'All right,' he said. 'Let's go and find out what's going on.'

We went out into the corridor and began making our way to the fifth floor of the western side of the building. The corridors seemed as dimly lighted by day as they had by night ... the daylight streaming through the thin windows was wan and cool. The day was overcast and sombre.

We passed a number of people in the corridors – mostly young people, presumably students in training for the élite. They watched us as we passed, alertly but incuriously. We must have been the dominant topic of conversation among them for days.

There were more people in the radio room. In fact, there was quite a crowd there. One of them moved to cut off the doorway as we approached, but big though he was he couldn't block the view. His action had been reflexive in any case, for as we peered past him he thought better of it, and moved aside.

The people within were picking through the wreckage.

To the man who had attempted to block our way, I said, 'Who did it?'

'Jason, Lucas ... perhaps a dozen others.' He was hesitant, but his hesitancy was born of anxiety rather than any reluctance to let us in on the secret. He seemed almost glad we were there, as if it were a relief to have someone with whom to share the responsibility for the discovery. Presumably, the authority he would normally have notified of any untoward incident was Jason, or Lucas ... or any of the others in the administrative group. When you find that the law has committed a crime, where do you turn?

'Where are they now?' I asked, taking advantage of the fact that answers were easy to come by, for once.

'They went to the mainland,' said the giant. 'They took all the boats but two ... and the others are damaged, sinking in the harbour.'

'It seems,' said Nathan, still monumentally unperturbed by the whole chain of events, 'that Jason is not a man to do things by halves. He's done a comprehensive job of cutting us off from the mainland. He appears to have won himself time, if nothing else.'

'Time to do *what*?' I demanded.

But he ignored the question. Instead, he asked the Florian whether the Planners had been informed. The idea of interrupting the Planners in the course of their affairs was obviously not a welcome one so far as the young man was concerned. Among the acolytes in the aristocracy presumptive, if nowhere else, the Planners preserved their status as demigods.

'You'd better make sure they're informed,' said Nathan gently.

As he turned away, I said, 'What do *we* do?'

'We go back to my room,' he said, 'and we wait. I know you don't like it, but there's nothing we can do. I think the Planners will tell us what's going on in due course, and perhaps invite us into their council. In the meantime, we take things easy.'

There was, as he said, nothing we could do. What I found offensive, however, was not his insistence on making this clear but his apparent contentment with it.

The sensation of being completely helpless is – at least so far as I am concerned – one of the most painful in the range of human experience. It is one with which, perhaps, I was always overfamiliar. Those who allow themselves to perceive the everyday tragedies that occur perpetually in the world around them live in a constant state of excited awareness, and when the wheel of chance brings such tragedies so closely as to make personal contact the fury of impotence can become overwhelming.

That afternoon and evening, I could not help envying Nathan his detachment – his lack of emotional involvement even with events happening to him and around him. I could not help, also, a degree of insight into the way Arne Jason had been pricked into hasty – and perhaps violent – action by the conspiracy of circumstances. He was not angry because he had lost anything real, but he had lost his pretensions, his illusions, the cloak of pretence which had kept him isolated from the impact of feeling his own impotence to control and direct the pattern of events. As Nathan had said, the Planners were aware of him, were manipulating him even while he believed himself to be manipulating them: a tissue of ambivalence maintained by mutual consent. And now ... we had denied him. And all of a sudden, he was at the head of a revolution.

How, I wondered, were the Planners to cope with the rebellion? How could they possibly suppress it? If Jason and his new allies were to take control of the colony by force – as, perhaps, they already had – what could the Planners do? There was no question of their fighting back ... for that was precisely what they stood implacably against. On a world where violence has been banished, what conceivable defence is there against it?

I not only felt personally helpless, but conceived of us all as being helpless. So far as I could see, we were at the mercy of Jason's injured pride. I recalled the day when my son's mother had been killed, in a random traffic accident that was part of a great pattern of random accidents extending across all the roads of the world and all the hours of the day and night. I had not even been in the same country when it happened, and though she lived a while in the hospital there was no way I could have travelled fast enough to reach her before she died. But if there had been – if there had been a device like the *Daedalus*, to translocate me in spacetime with negligible delay – I could have done nothing save wait for her to die, at the whim of a pattern of events without sense or order.

In my head, I live in an ordered universe of cause and effect and the eternal, immutable principles of natural law. But real events in the real world are not subject to the same constraints as the universe of thought inside any man's head, and we are all at the mercy of the unpredictable.

Even Mariel, to whom no lies could be told.

CHAPTER SEVENTEEN

I lay in my bed, having abandoned the attempt to sleep. My eyes were open but I could see nothing. A heavy curtain cut out such light as might have crept in through the window, and the corridor outside, with the nearest stairwell some distance away, was too dark to make a rim of light around the ill-fitting door.

I heard the door open and close again, but though I was fully conscious I did not react. I waited, while whoever had entered moved across the carpet to my side. I was conscious of the presence only a foot or two away from my face, but still I waited.

A hand groped for my shoulder, and a voice whispered, 'Mr Alexander.'

I was surprised to hear my name given thus. I had assumed, though without any real reason, that the invader was either Karen or Nathan. I was so prepared to hear one of their voices, in fact, that I couldn't put a name to the voice I did hear. I knew that I knew it, but I couldn't place it.

I felt the hand gripping my shoulder and stirring me gently. It was a large hand.

'Wake up, Mr Alexander,' said the voice.

And then I recognised it.

I sat bolt upright with a suddenness that must have startled him.

'*Rondo?*'

'Quietly, Mr Alexander,' he said. 'I'll turn on the light.'

After a pause, the light came on. It was, indeed, the youngest of the Planners. The devil's advocate.

'What do you want?' I demanded harshly. But I kept my voice low.

He came swiftly back to the bedside, and knelt down. 'You know that I had to question you this afternoon,' he said. 'It is my function. There was nothing personal. Perhaps your colleague told you that I was, myself, disposed to be sympathetic?'

'So?' I said.

'I want your help, Mr Alexander,' he said.

'What kind of help?'

'I want to go to the mainland. Tonight.'

I didn't say anything. I just stared at him, completely out of my depth.

'You have a boat, Mr Alexander,' he said. 'The one you used in order to get here. You have hidden it somewhere on the island. I think you have probably contemplated using it yourself.'

'It had crossed my mind,' I admitted. 'But there's a moratorium on bull-in-a-china-shop tactics. And I have blisters on my hands.'

He smiled. He didn't look like a Planner. He was younger than Jason, but built along the same lines. Immensely strong . . . it was hard to imagine him as a die-hard pacifist.

'I'll row,' he said.

'You want me to go with you?'

He nodded. 'I need your help,' he said again.

I looked briefly at the door. 'Very quiet help,' I said, with slight sarcasm.

'Very quiet,' he agreed.

There were a hundred questions, chief among which was, 'What the hell are you playing at?' – but I didn't ask them. I got out of bed. Whatever he wanted to do, it was action, and I felt the need for action in every muscle of my body. I'd had a rough time, and I'd gone distinctly short of sleep these last few days, but I needed little urging. The compulsion to do something – *anything* except wait in silent helplessness – was irresistible.

He seemed slightly amused by my readiness, but he was also pleased. When I was dressed, he turned out the light and opened the door. I followed him, on tiptoe, as he led me through the maze of passages to a small door on the inland side of the building. Once outside, he brought forth a small lantern – not an electric torch but a candle mounted in a glass case. It seemed oddly out of place here, at the very heart of Florian technological expertise. But there are no such things as levels of technology: only matters of convenience and priority.

'Where's the boat?' he asked.

'At the foot of the cliff,' I said. 'We'd better take the long way around.'

He shook his head. 'I know a safe path.'

I wasn't sure. The light cast by the sheltered candle was too faint to light our way adequately. But I followed him, and took great care to tread exactly where he trod. He preceded me, so that if I did slip I would have to fall past him.

It took no more than ten minutes to get down to the pebbled shore, and only five minutes more to find the boat under the ledge where I'd left it.

We pulled it out, and manoeuvered it into the water. Rondo took both oars in a single massive fist, and held the boat steady while I stepped in. He was about to follow me when the sound of footsteps on the loose stones made us both look back.

It was, inevitably, Karen Karelia. We'd passed her room in the corridor. She had, it seemed, been no more asleep than I. She seemed surprised and alarmed to recognise Rondo. She had known, obviously, that it was a Florian I was with, but this must have been the first opportunity for her to see his face. He, however, seemed both unsurprised and unperturbed by her arrival.

'What's going on?' she asked – of me.

'I don't know,' I told her. '*He's* in charge.'

'Get in the boat,' said Rondo calmly.

She got in the boat. Rondo pushed us away from the shore and then began to put the oars into the rowlocks. We took up a position in the stern, facing him as he began to pull us around in a semicircle, and then, with a few casual strokes of the oars, sent us shooting away from the island.

'The others aren't going to like it when they find out,' I commented.

'I think,' he said, 'that this is one of those times when it's better to act first and discuss the matter later.'

'I'm astonished to find one of the Planners believing that there ever could be such a time,' I said.

'Where are we going?' asked Karen. 'And why?'

'I know Arne Jason,' said Rondo smoothly. 'I know him better, perhaps, than anyone else. The others, you see, are all older than he. When they knew him as a boy, they were already adult. When *I* knew him as a boy, I was his junior. That can be a very different viewpoint. The others think that Jason is unimportant, dispensable. They look down upon him from their lofty place and they only see that in the long run he can achieve very little. They have toyed with him too long. They're right, of course, about the long run. But in a more immediate sense, Jason is a dangerous man.'

It came as a blessed relief to know that someone had noticed.

'So what do you intend to do about him?' I asked.

'Find him,' replied the Planner. 'Stay with him, if I can. And try to prevent him from doing any real harm.'

'By force?' asked Karen.

The candle was on the floor of the boat, and we could not see his face by its light. I could not guess what kind of expression he might be wearing. But his voice, when he answered, was nothing like the voice he might have used to react to such a question in his capacity as the spokesman for the Planners.

He simply said, 'Not by force.'

'I don't see what you think you can achieve,' she said bluntly.

'We'll see,' he said, in neutral tones.

'Why bring us?' I asked. 'You wanted me along, and you didn't send Karen back. But if you're so afraid of the consequences our actions may have – pollution of your cultural values, or however you want to put it – why invite us to the party? You didn't just volunteer to bring me so that I'd show you where the boat was.'

'I want you to guide me to your ship,' he said. 'And I want you to come to an agreement with Jason.'

'A deal?'

'If you like.'

'What *kind* of deal?'

'An honest deal, Mr Alexander. You have to make him see the kind of sense which you threw at us this afternoon. You have to make him realise that there are things more important than his personal ambitions.'

'Sweet reason?' I said, without conviction. 'What makes you think he'll listen? What makes you think he'll care?'

'He's a Florian,' said Rondo. 'The son of a colonial culture.'

'He didn't stay to listen today,' I pointed out. 'He isn't in a mood to believe the truth. He might not be ready to see reason; in fact, I'd say he's almost ready to react against it. He's a desperate man.'

'In that case,' said Rondo, again with quiet confidence, 'then we must show him up for what he is. We must let those he commands – and those with whom he has allied himself – see him for what he is.'

I could still hear Nathan's mocking advice ringing in my ears. *Be realistic*, he had said. And I had rejected, inwardly, his brand of realism. But how realistic was Rondo's belief that force could be opposed without force? How realistic was the conviction that Jason, Vulgan, and men like them could be turned aside from their objective with nothing more than words? They were, as Rondo had said, colonists and the sons of colonists. Men of Floria, who *must*, in their hearts, feel something of the ideals that had motivated their forefathers. But how much? To what extent had that idealism been eroded and repressed by the kind of cynical detachment which came so easy to us, the invaders from Earth? How powerful, I wondered, are time and circumstance?

There was no way of knowing. We were at the mercy of the unpredictable, with only Rondo's faith to guide us. Faith, I knew, can be a very unsatisfactory guide. Ask any of its victims.

'For some time,' said Rondo, 'we have anticipated this moment of rebellion. We had not expected it so soon ... perhaps, unconsciously, we hoped that it would never come, or believed that we could hold it at bay forever. Now that it is here, we are afraid, anxious, hesitant. We are not really attuned to the acceptance of new information – we live on the assumption of our virtual omniscience. What you have tried to make us see is something we are, for the most part, reluctant to confront. We are confused. I don't know how you think of us, but you must make allowances. You must try to realise the extent of the effect your coming here has had. It has been a shock.'

While he spoke he continued to haul on the oars with a steady rhythm. He seemed quite tireless. His voice remained perfectly level and composed. He breathed easily.

'You arrive,' he continued, 'at an awkward time. It is not so long ago – perhaps only a generation – that the rebellion you have touched off could not have happened. For six generations, the measure of a man on Floria was the measure of what he could make with his hands. Everything that a man had in the world was made directly by his own hands, or bought with the produce of his own hands. But over the years this has become gradually less true. What one generation has built, the next has inherited. Needs have, over the years, been supplied ... and the means to supply them have been sophisticated to the point at which it is no longer necessary for every man to spend his life making things in order to supply the needs of the people. As we have made our wealth, so we have allowed control of that wealth to pass gradually from the men who make it to the men who distribute it. The power of that wealth can be acquired, concentrated ... and the measure of a man changes from what he has made and can make to what he has bought and can buy. And because of this the absolute command enjoyed by the Planners has steadily declined. We are no longer directly responsible for sustaining the life of the colony. The people can live their own lives, supply their own needs. Do you see what I mean?'

'I see what you're getting at,' I told him. 'At first, life was hard. You came out of your tin cans with nothing but the clothes you stood up in and a few domestic animals. Ever since then you've been battling to survive. But now, you're surviving. You've built what you set out to build. *Your* plans go much further into the future, but people like Vulgan now have the latitude to make their own plans. . . . The devil finds work for idle hands.'

'Not the devil, Mr Alexander,' he said gently. 'It's not evil we have to face, but opportunism. What's happening is quite natural.'

'Then what makes you think you can stop it?' said Karen. 'They never managed it back on Earth. Not in three thousand years.'

'We began life here with little more than our bare hands,' said Rondo. 'But we did not begin as savages. We began as intelligent men and women – the product of a civilisation which had equipped our minds, if not our bodies. The first colonists were in a position to learn and recognise not only the value, but the *necessity*, of co-operation and co-ordination.'

'Never mind that crap,' said Karen, lacking in subtlety but cutting to the heart of the matter. 'Just tell us how, without the use of force, you intend to put down this rebellion.'

'We don't,' he said. 'Not in the sense that you mean.'

'What other sense is there?' she demanded.

'There's no reason at all why we should try to stop Ellerich and Vulgan claiming new titles and setting up new structures of government,' said Rondo. 'We're not interested in that kind of exercise. What is going on at the moment is that all the men we have educated on the island – and perhaps half a dozen that we have not – are sorting themselves out into those who are prepared to join Ellerich's challenge and those who are not. I presume that those who are not will be placed under arrest. In order to be successful Ellerich needs to win the greater number to his own side – but the more he wins the more dilute his cause becomes. The more support he tries to win, the more compromises he will have to make. And he is working, you must remember, with men that we have trained, men that we have tried to infect with our ideas. No matter how many ideas of their own they have acquired, they remain, at heart, our men . . . accepting our aims if not our methods.

'The more success Ellerich's rebellion wins in recruiting supporters, the less powerful will be the force of his own self-seeking determination. We can't stop this rebellion ... but we have been working to subvert it for more than a hundred years. We will allow Ellerich to prepare his demands, and we will give in to some of them from the very start. Then we will begin to talk about the rest. And we will keep talking, preserving and acting within a slowly changing balance of power ... for a hundred years, and a thousand. We don't need totalitarian control in order to direct the course of history. All we need is to preserve something of the monopoly we have on knowledge. That monopoly will be eroded, but very slowly. By the time it has gone completely, it will no longer be necessary.'

'You're assuming,' I said, 'that the rebels will talk – will permit themselves to become enmeshed in a process of slow change, bogged down in endless argument. Suppose they simply elect to storm your citadel and take control of all the microfilms and whatever that were brought from Earth?'

'Perhaps they will,' said the Planner. 'Perhaps they'll raze the library to the ground and burn everything – Planners, Plans, and all. Perhaps they'll restore the innocent and forceful rule of barbarism. But we have to believe that they won't ... that they didn't come here as barbarians, and that we have achieved *something* in all these years in predisposing them to talk rather than to burn. Ellerich needs support, you see, and the more support he recruits the more our influence will show in his followers. I don't think they'll want to use force.'

'All the assumptions are very fine,' I said. 'But the presence of one committed, desperate man could make a lot of difference. Just one man who *is*, despite everything you've done here, a savage man, determined that his way, and his way alone, is the way the colony has to go. One man could take your carefully balanced situation apart.'

'Only if he could persuade others to act with him and for him,' insisted Rondo.

'You have no idea,' I told him, 'how easy persuasion can be when you have a gun.'

'*Has* Jason got a gun?' interrupted Karen.

'Has he?' I said, to Rondo.

'I don't know,' said the youngest of the Planners. 'But you could be right. That's why we're going to the mainland. To stop Arne Jason. But not by force. If we can't win him, then we must win his supporters. He is, as you say, the main danger ... one committed man ... but he cannot stand alone, armed or not.'

I only hoped he was right. But if he was so damned certain, why were we here? Why didn't we just sit on the island and wait for it all to come up roses?

It seemed that even the Planners – one of them, at least – recognised the power of the unpredictable.

CHAPTER EIGHTEEN

We made for a point to the south of Leander. Had we gone to the north we'd have had to cope with the outflow of the river as well as the salt marsh. Rondo's intention was to be as unobtrusive as was practical, coming into the town on foot from the south rather than pulling into the harbour and attracting immediate attention. In the town, we could get horses and ride over the country to the ship. There, we hoped, we might find Jason ... and if we failed to find Jason we could at least find out what was happening throughout the colony.

The young giant was still showing no sign of undue exertion as he hauled us in to the shore. I took up the lighted candle from the floor of the boat and stepped out, holding it up so that we could see where we were. Rondo moored the boat.

The shore consisted of moss-covered rocks interspersed with tussocks of coarse grass. There were a few bushes close to the shore, and an extensive wood about a hundred yards inland. We began to walk northwards along the shore, making our way carefully over the rough ground.

We were so careful, in fact, that we walked right into their arms. There were five of them, waiting in line while we came to them. They were carrying no light, but as we reached them one of them lit a small lantern similar to our own.

'Well, Mr Alexander,' said Carl Vulgan. 'We've been expecting you. But I don't know your friend from the island. And I was never properly introduced to the young lady.'

I didn't feel like making introductions. 'We should have blown out the damned candle,' I murmured, wondering what Vulgan was doing deploying half Leander's police force to pick us up. Obviously, Rondo wasn't the only one who'd remembered our boat.

'It wouldn't have made any difference,' Vulgan assured us. 'We have men up in the tall trees. It's remarkable how easy it is to see a boat cutting through the sea-shimmer ... provided that you know what you're looking for.'

'And Jason told you what to look for?'

'Oh, yes.' Vulgan seemed extremely self-satisfied. He figured that he held all the cards. Maybe he did.

'So what now?' I asked.

But he didn't answer. He was eyeing Rondo speculatively.

'My name's Ewan Rondo,' said the Planner.

'It doesn't matter,' said Vulgan. 'We'll have to place you under arrest. Anyone, you see, coming from the island is likely to cause us trouble. Unless, of course, you want to join us?'

'No,' said Rondo, perhaps unwisely.

'You're making a mistake,' I told Vulgan.

'I don't think so,' he replied.

'Jason's trying to use you in exactly the same way that you tried to use me. He hasn't joined you, he's trying to take you over.'

'We all want the same thing,' said Vulgan calmly.

'Where's Jason now?' I asked. 'In Leander?'

'He's negotiating with the people aboard your ship.'

'And what does "negotiating" mean? Threatening to kill Mariel if the ship doesn't either open up or get out? He doesn't realise what he's doing. You *need* the ship, desperately. You can't just arrest us and put us out of the way while

157

Jason plays his stupid games. Rolving won't surrender, but if Jason tries anything silly, like putting dynamite under her, then he might take her up ... and she can't stay in orbit long. You've got to let us sort this thing out.'

'I've no intention of placing *you* under arrest, Mr Alexander,' said Vulgan. 'What would be the point? You came here to deal with the government ... and now we *are* the government. From today, the Planners are effectively powerless. You are completely free to go where you wish ... and we will be pleased to provide you with transport. That applies to yourself and Miss Karelia, but not, I'm afraid, to *you*.'

Rondo appeared to take this with the utmost serenity.

'Suppose I want to go back to the island?' I asked.

Vulgan shrugged. 'If you wish,' he said. 'But what would be the point? Unless, of course, you wish to collect the remaining member of your party.'

I contemplated that, knowing that Nathan would never forgive me if he found out I'd had a chance to go back, and then shook my head.

'I want to go to the ship,' I said. 'I want to make sure Jason doesn't do anything stupid. And I want to make sure Mariel's all right – and stays all right.'

'There's a train tomorrow morning,' said the police chief.

'Damn the train,' I said. 'Isn't there a faster way?'

'If you can ride a horse. But it's not a good road to ride at night.'

'I can ride,' I said. 'And I'll risk it.'

'So will I,' said Karen.

Vulgan looked at her, then at me. He seemed amused. He turned to one of the waiting policemen and told him to bring three of the horses. 'It seems that the rest of us will be walking home,' he commented, with heavy irony. 'But it's not far. I presume that you have no objection to my allowing one of my officers to guide you? It would be so easy for you to lose your way.'

I opened my mouth to reply, but Rondo cut in quickly and smoothly. 'He's right, Mr Alexander. Let the officer guide you. I'll try to sort out matters here. I'll explain the situation as you explained it to us. Talk to Jason. Come to terms with him. Remember what I said to you in the boat.'

I hesitated. There was no note of appeal in his voice, nor any attempt to command me. He was leaving it in my hands. He had an awful lot of faith for a man who'd been suggesting not ten hours ago that I was a powerful subversive influence, a threat to the whole Florian dream. Maybe what he was doing would have horrified most of the Planners. Maybe he was a fool. But as he stood there and spoke so evenly, I couldn't help feeling that we were under obligation to him. For a whole host of reasons, most of which I felt rather than thought.

'I'll talk to him,' I promised. 'I'll do what I can. No crowbars.'

'Thank you,' he said. He might, I thought, have to withdraw that at a later date.

We waited, while one of the policemen led three horses from the trees. Vulgan told him where the ship was, and suggested a route. His parting words were along the lines of, 'See that you deliver them safely.' Then he, with the rest of his men, escorted Rondo back along the shore towards Leander.

With some trepidation, I approached the gargantuan mount. I couldn't even get on top of it without help from the policeman. I knew that whatever else came of this lunatic jaunt I was going to be extremely saddle-sore.

Once the uniformed giant had managed to get us both into the saddle he led us slowly through the trees to the dirt road which cut through the western corner of the wood and extended directly to the south. Once there, the pace picked up to a trot.

One of the privileges of being a UN biologist is that one is not merely *allowed* into those areas of Earthly wilderness which are specifically set aside as preservation regions but quite often *ordered* into them for various reasons. Sometimes it is to investigate by indirect means whether or not their sanctity is being violated, more often it is because they are the only places left on Earth where observational data concerning 'natural' processes may be obtained. Everywhere else – including national parks and local conservation areas –

the degree of human interference is so great that one can no longer assume that the behaviour of species is unaffected by human activity.

The advantage of having periodically adventured in fully qualified wilderness is quite simply that the only way to travel in such regions – the only way one is permitted to travel – is on horseback. Thus, when faced with the prospect of a long ride through the night along dirt roads, I was not at a loss. The horse was large, but it was good-tempered and was used to being sat upon by a variety of riders. I had no idea what previous experience with horses Karen might have had, but suspected that she was hanging on more by will-power than skill. She gritted her teeth and believed that all would be well, and fate probably lacked the courage to contradict her.

Our guide did not exactly set a blistering pace, but I was content to take it relatively easy. We had a long way to go, and even if the horses were as tireless as the people they were going to be pushed quite hard enough without being pressed forward at a gallop. In any case, the syndrome which had allowed them to grow large had probably robbed them of any capacity they might have had for real speed. They seemed exceptionally solidly built in the legs.

The road did not keep a straight course for long but was forced to wind and dip following valleys through the hills where we had earlier sought refuge. It veered right and left, seeking out each tiny outcrop of civilisation – villages, and even single farmhouses.

The night was clear, and the stars shone now in their greatest profusion. Periodically, as we passed through wooded areas, the light would be blocked almost entirely, but even when we could not see our way, the mounts seemed sure-footed and confident. I was shivering with the cold, however, and my hands were numb as they gripped the reins.

My mind slipped easily back into a mechanical laxity, with my body continuing while my consciousness lapsed into a state of semi-awareness. I was like a spring unwinding at a measured rate, controlled by inner tensions. The journey seemed interminable, but never intolerable. Thanks to some of the habits gathered during my lifetime, I knew the value of patience. One can't be familiar with the needs of scientific observation without learning that things take their own time no matter how much we urge them. It may not always be better to travel hopefully than to arrive, but with practice it is usually easier on the mind.

In the early part of the journey, our guide (or guard) led the way, but by the time the dawn chorus would have been sounding had there been sufficient Earthly birds imported to the colony, I had taken the lead. The policeman had dropped back some way, and only when I stopped because I was doubtful of our direction did he catch up. The reason for this was simply that his horse was carrying twice the load, and was suffering more than mine or Karen's. I contemplated trying to shake him altogether, and could no doubt have done so, but I saw no point. There was nothing covert about our intentions. In fact, I had a vague suspicion that the bigger the crowd might be when we finally confronted Jason, the better the chance I might have of persuading him that there were no dividends for getting tough.

We rode into the village from the north just as the sun had climbed above the horizon. We crossed the small bridge over the stream and walked the horses casually past the hall where we had been entertained on our first night down. A number of people were already up and about, and though they stopped to stare at us they didn't seem particularly surprised. I didn't see anyone I knew.

The hall was deserted, but I hadn't really expected to find Jason or any of his men there. They'd be out at Joe Saccone's farmhouse, letting the village get on with its everyday business in its everyday way.

Karen came up abreast while the policeman was still some way back.

'What now?' she asked.

'Take it easy,' I said. 'I'd like to see Harwin, if he's around.'

'Why?' she wanted to know.

'Moral support.'

'What makes you think that he'll morally support you against Jason?'

I shrugged. 'He didn't like the way Jason took us off his hands. He's an honest man. I know we're outsiders, but if Jason intends any dirty tricks, I'd like to have half a dozen honest witnesses around.'

But Harwin was nowhere to be seen. It wasn't really surprising. He'd probably be getting on with his honest work somewhere out in the fields. I could have located him, but what reason could I give for dragging him away?

The cop arrived, and paused. He looked at us questioningly. I considered his face. It wasn't handsome – the expanded faces of the Florians all looked rather repellent to me – but it wasn't aggressive or cruel.

'The ship's that way,' I told him, pointing.

He nodded, and waited. He obviously intended to stay with us all the way. He was welcome, so far as I was concerned.

I let the horse carry me forward again, feeling the ache in my thighs as I moved slightly, knowing that I was going to be feeling it for some time to come, and hoping that I'd be able to stand up and walk when I got down again.

'I wish I didn't feel as if I were walking right into a shark's jaws,' commented Karen.

I felt exactly the same way.

CHAPTER NINETEEN

They saw us coming, and were waiting for us.

I felt very shaky as I dismounted at the gate, and it took me several seconds to find my legs. I paused for a good while before opening the gate and moving inside, with Karen and the cop right behind me.

The yard in front of the house was bordered by barns and

pig-sties. There were a couple of men in the shadow of the barn door, watching us as we marched across the open space. There was no sign of Joe Saccone or his wife and children, and though the pigs were making just as much noise as pigs usually do, it seemed preternaturally quiet.

Jason came out of the house as we approached. There was another man with him – a well-dressed, self-assured man.

My eyes met and joined with Jason's while we were still a long way apart. Some time passed before my hesitant stride consumed the distance between us. Eventually, however, we stood face to face. I had to look up at him. He looked like a cat confronted by a mouse with its hind legs tied.

'We didn't expect you so soon,' he said.

'You shouldn't have left in such a hurry,' I said. 'We could have come with you.'

'Did the rowing hurt your hands?'

'Not in the least,' I assured him. 'One of the Planners rowed us across. He's talking to Vulgan now.'

His smugness didn't slip.

'I'd like to see Mariel,' I said, when he didn't reply. 'Then I'd like to go back to my ship. We can discuss the situation when I'm certain that everyone is safe.'

It was an optimistic suggestion.

'Come in,' he said.

Both men stood aside while I passed between them. Karen followed me into the house, but they moved to exclude the policeman. He looked bewildered for a moment, but didn't turn away. I don't think it was duty so much as curiosity that impelled him forward. He brushed past Jason and got in.

Once the door had closed behind the well-dressed man, the main room of the house was pretty crowded. The farmer's wife was watching from the kitchen door. Mariel was sitting in an armchair beside the newly set fire that burned in the grate. Standing beside her was Lucas.

And Lucas had a gun.

Behind me, Jason leaned to pick something up, and when I turned he had a gun as well. They weren't sophisticated firearms by any means – they looked like a cross between a sawed-off shotgun and a blunderbuss – but someone had put them together with loving care and was very proud of them. There were no prizes for guessing who.

I'd feared this, and also half expected it.

'What's that for?' I asked, pointing at the one Jason held. I knew damn well what it was for. I also knew that the sheer pride in having brought it into the world was likely to go to Jason's head. A man who brings an engine of destruction into a world where such things are unknown is bound to have an exaggerated idea of its efficacy and worth. I knew that irrespective of which course was wisest or most likely to get him something of what he wanted, Jason was going to try to use that gun to get it all. But what did he want, now?

'Don't worry about the gun,' he said. 'It won't go off. If you're sensible.'

It wasn't hard to tell that he was new at the game. The words were from way back. And so was the thought behind them.

I walked over to Mariel.

'Are you all right?' I asked.

She nodded. 'They didn't lock me up,' she said quietly. 'But there was nowhere to run. I didn't expect the guns. The men here watching the ship didn't know about them.'

'It's OK,' I said. There wasn't much point in trying to reassure her further. She knew as well as I did that I was worried.

I turned, and pointed at the stranger. 'Who's he?' I said to Jason.

But the stranger spoke for himself. 'My name is Paul Ellerich,' he said.

'Congratulations,' I said. 'I hear you just inherited a planet. Or has Jason already disabused you of the notion?'

'We're on the same side,' said Jason smoothly. 'We want the same thing and we have it within the palms of our hands. All we have to do is take it.'

'The thing between the palms of his hands,' I said, aiming the words at Ellerich, 'is a gun. And he intends to rule you with it just like the rest of the world.'

Ellerich wasn't impressed.

'Well,' I said, redirecting my attention to Jason. 'What's the deal now? Do you still want us to get out and leave you to it?'

He shook his head. 'Not now,' he said.

'What *do* you want?'

'I want control over your ship, and I want control over everything your party does while it remains here. You will work for us, Mr Alexander, and not for the Planners. And *we* will decide how vital you are to the future of this colony, and in what way you may help us.'

'And how do you intend to exercise that control?' I asked politely.

'I want both your pilots to surrender themselves as hostages. We will look after them – and the little girl – very well, until it is time for you to leave. In the meantime, you will do as we ask.'

I glanced briefly at Mariel, wondering how he knew that we had only two people capable of handling the ship. But we hadn't made any secret of the number and make-up of the ship's personnel when we'd first landed.

'We can't do that,' I said quietly. I had to remember that it was time to be diplomatic.

The only trouble was that Jason had already abandoned his diplomatic pretensions. He was determined.

'You have no choice,' he told me. 'We've already issued an ultimatum to the ship. If your people within don't surrender before noon, then we use the guns.'

'Mariel,' I said casually. 'Is he bluffing?'

Jason was confused for a moment, but he didn't say anything.

'I don't know,' replied Mariel. 'I don't think he does, either.'

It wasn't a very helpful reply.

'There's no need for unpleasantness,' Ellerich intervened. 'The simple fact is that we now control this colony. You have no alternative but to deal with us. And we have the right to determine what you will do while you are here.'

'Then why do it at the point of a gun?' I demanded.

'We have to make sure of your co-operation. The internal

difficulties of the colony are not going to be settled overnight. We cannot let you work with the Planners against us . . . and that is what you have tried to do. You must not help to sustain the situation which leaves the Planners in effective control of Floria. You must, instead, help us to break their stranglehold. We cannot take any risks . . . you must do as we ask.'

'We'll co-operate with you to the best of our ability,' I said. 'But you must let us all return to the ship. There will be no hostages taken.'

'You're behind the times,' said Jason, in a voice that grated slightly with implied threat. 'We already have hostages. Three of you. What we want is recognition of that fact and capitulation. No doubt your ship can take off and go home right now . . . but what good would that do any of us? You'd still be here, still in a position to give us much of the information we want . . . but not, perhaps, in a position to help us as fully as *you* might wish. Be reasonable, Mr Alexander . . . if the ship takes off, everybody suffers. If you do as you're told, we can all gain.'

'Only yesterday,' I said, 'you were trying to persuade me to clear out altogether. Now you want me to stay. What's changed, in the meantime? Why were we all to suffer yesterday, whereas now we're all to gain? The difference is that you've changed sides. The only thing that concerns you is *your* gain. Nobody else's. It wouldn't have bothered you yesterday if I'd agreed to your proposition, and in consequence the whole colony and all of its people would have suffered for generations to come. You didn't stay to hear what I had to say to the Planners – to hear *why* our presence here is vital to your health, and perhaps your survival. Why not? Because you weren't interested. You didn't want to know what kind of trouble this colony is in and what we can do to help you . . . you only wanted to get a head start on us, smashing the radio, sinking the boats, so that you'd have time to shift all your eggs to a different basket. As soon as we threatened your position with the Planners, you decided you'd find a new position with the rebels. You don't give a damn about the prospect of the colonists as long as you can be the man on top. You don't care who holds notional control as long as you're the man who controls *them*.'

I turned to Ellerich and continued. 'Is this the kind of man you want to run your revolution? Is this the man you'd like to have pulling your strings? The Planners thought that while he was working for them they could keep him in check – a balance of power in which he thought he was controlling them and they thought they were controlling him. Is that what you think? Or are you just going along with him because what's good for his personal ambitions looks like being good for yours? How many years do you think he'll give you before that gun is pointed at you? You know his methods . . . you're watching them in operation right now. Is this really the way you want to set things right here?'

Ellerich didn't answer. But I knew he had to be wondering. He had to be in doubt as to whether he'd jumped the right way. Until yesterday, Jason had been the enemy. Today he was the crucial ally. But even a saint would have his cynical suspicions. The thing was, could Ellerich control Jason? What could he do, now, except go along? It was Jason who was holding the gun. Ellerich, like every other man on Floria, must have a quasi-supernatural regard for the weapon. He didn't know much about them but he knew they were terrible enough to be a dread secret. He *believed* in the awesome power of the gun . . . and while Jason controlled it, he was likely to stick with Jason. At a later date, of course, he might get one of his own, at which time things might be different, but until then . . .

I could see the whole thing unfolding into the alternate realms of possibility. The Planners' attempt to alter human nature and redirect the course of human history looked pretty sick at this particular moment. All it took was one committed man . . . one man who wasn't even sure whether he was bluffing or not, who had faith in his power even though there was no way he could estimate its extent. All it took was one messiah of the gun . . . and a lot of converts, a host of believers.

When the silence had gone on just long enough, Jason spoke again. 'You have no alternative,' he said, pressing his point hard. 'Either you do what we say, or you do nothing at all. You may even die.'

I glanced back at the policeman who'd brought us here, and I looked at Joe Saccone's wife, still hovering half out of sight by the kitchen door. I even looked at Lucas. I would have liked to know that *someone* was listening.

'This is what the Planners have worked seven generations trying to save you from,' I said, directing my comments into the empty air. 'Guns spit hot metal. They kill people. They kill you just as dead as poison, but quicker.'

I dried up. I couldn't think of any more. It didn't seem to be any use. They didn't know what the hell I was talking about. Not even Jason. They didn't come from Earth. They were Florians, with some kind of unreachable innocence protecting them from all the bitterness I was trying to show them.

It was pointless.

Jason gripped his weapon purposefully. He was aiming it at me. I was talking too much. He was just about pig sick of me. Maybe sick enough to shoot.

'I want you to talk to your pilot,' he said. 'Tell him to surrender the ship. Now. The ultimatum is running out.'

My mouth was dry. I wanted to protest the fact that I couldn't give Rolving orders and even if I could he wouldn't have obeyed them. I wanted to say that there was no way at all they could force or seduce their way into the *Daedalus*. I wanted to make Jason understand that it was all futile.

Instead, I simply said, 'No.'

I knew that it wasn't the way Nathan Parrick would have gone about it, and I was almost certain that Rondo would have found another way. But there was only one way I could see, and though it scared me very badly, it seemed to be the only way I could go.

Jason moved half a stride closer. Imperceptibly, the men on either side of him moved back. 'I'll kill you, Mr Alexander,' he said.

He was mad at me. Absurdly, I thought that in the old melodramas you could always get out of a situation like this by insulting the bad guy's courage and shaming him into fighting you barehanded. Then you licked the hell out of him. Only Jason was seven feet tall and his bare hands could have broken me as easily as the shot in his crude firearm.

'So kill me,' I said, feeling about ready to keel over and die anyway. My heart was going like a train and I was afraid my legs would start shaking any second.

'Tell him, Miss Valory, since you're so very clever, whether I know whether I'm bluffing now,' said Jason. It was a clumsy sentence but his tongue didn't stumble once.

'I think he intends to shoot,' said Mariel softly.

There are times when a lie detector is a liability.

'You'd better do as I say,' said Jason. 'Unless the more recent wonders of Earthly science included a technique for resurrecting the dead.'

'We haven't found anything like that,' I said, surprised by the levelness of my voice. 'But things *have* changed in two hundred years. Abilities ... and attitudes. There are new medical methods ... and there are also new beliefs. And maybe the beliefs are almost as important as the methods. I have a son back on Earth who believes, among other things, that Earth ought to be made into a better world before we try to build better worlds among the stars. He wants to make Earth into the kind of planet that the Planners – and perhaps most of the people – would like to see Floria become. On Earth, the job seems rather more difficult, for any number of reasons; one of which is that on Earth gun use and gun logic are already endemic. But my son subscribes to a belief that the way to beat a gun is not to give in to it. He believes that to render a gun powerless, you have to say *no*.

'On Earth, every day – I don't know how many times – people get threatened with guns. A lot of them say *no*, because they believe it's the only way. A lot of them get shot, still believing that it's the only way. They believe that by getting shot they demonstrate that force has no power to compel ... only power to kill. A lot of people think my son's ideas are crazy. The faith to which he belongs is opposed by authority, and lives almost on the fringe of legality. That's a compliment . . . an acknowledgment that it may just work. It may be stupid . . . every man a potential martyr . . and it may not last out the century . . . and it may cost a hell of a lot of lives . . . but it may be the only way.

'If you're going to shoot, shoot. But what do you do for an encore?'

I thought I could talk him out of it. I really did. I thought I was being clever rather than brave. I couldn't believe that he was really so desperate.

'You're a fool,' he said, and raised the barrel of the gun slightly to aim at my ribs.

It's all so pointless, I thought. *You made all this trouble for yourself, out of your own vanity, your own crazy pretensions. You could have kept all the power that ever really meant anything. . . .*

He pressed the trigger.

And the gun blew apart in his hands.

I had spun away, my face turned and my arms coming up reflexively to shield me from the shot. I felt tiny stings in my shoulder, as if I had been attacked by a host of wasps. I went down, not realising what had happened. But I fell. I wasn't thrown backwards by the impact.

I was hit . . . but Jason was screaming and clawing at his face. The wreckage of the gun had been hurled aside by a convulsive jerk. There seemed to be blood everywhere. *His* blood.

I was curling up, but still conscious. I realised that I was alive and likely to stay that way. I could have laughed.

Jason was still alive, too, but it seemed something of a miracle. He seemed to have taken most of the explosive force in his face and upper chest, although he had held the stock of the gun no higher than his waist. He was thrashing convulsively in the grip of some chaotic chain of reflex. He would be in pain for a long, long time to come.

I felt Karen's hands on my shoulders. She was trying to help me up. I resisted.

Nobody else had moved, but at least one other person had screamed. I didn't know who.

I watched Lucas slowly relax the hands with which he

gripped his own gun. The barrel drooped and fell. Then he dropped it, and looked down at it with offended horror.

'The trouble with homemade guns and ammunition,' I said, in a remote voice, 'is that they can't be standardised properly. You're always likely to get a cartridge that explodes in the breech.'

There was another thought crossing my mind ... something about the mercy of the unpredictable ... but I couldn't form it. I had caught sight of my own blood, staining my sleeve deep red. It still hurt.

I fainted.

CHAPTER TWENTY

I woke up a couple of times before they finally got me back into the ship, but consciousness didn't seem like a good idea, and I wasn't sorry when Conrad finally put me out with a hypodermic. I think people kept reassuring me that everything was all right.

I slept for a long time, even after the drug had worn off. I was in a state of advanced exhaustion. A couple of days had gone by before I was eventually allowed to sit up and consume a little liquid nourishment by the conventional route. I was passed fit for visitors, but with the size of a starship cabin being what it is they had to come in one by one. It fell to Karen's lot to bring me up to date.

The first thing she did was to open my palm and dump half a dozen little metal pellets in it.

'What's that?' I asked her.

'The lead they took out of your shoulder,' she said. 'I thought you might like it as a souvenir of how close you came to being dead. You can get blood poisoning from that kind of thing, you know.'

I weighed the fragments in my hand. They came to no more than a couple of grams.

'They didn't go very deep,' she added. 'Insufficient thrust.'

'How much did we take out of Jason?' I inquired.

'About four times as much. A lot just distributed itself about the room. It was a big bullet.'

'Is Jason alive?'

'Oh, yes. On his way back to the hospital in Hope Landing. Scarred for life, though. And his hands will never be the same again. He'll be booked for a sedentary occupation from now on . . . and he'll likely run to fat.'

'And the situation in general?'

'Oh,' she said offhand, 'you saved that. All that melodrama didn't go to waste. Ellerich decided there had to be a better way. The talk is already starting. It'll go on for months. Very boring. Nathan's not back yet. He's got a lot of work in front of him.'

'So have we all,' I said. 'It's time to start catching rats.'

'You already caught a big one,' she said. 'But using yourself for bait is kind of dangerous. It was an almighty fluke that you didn't get your head blown off. You took one hell of a gamble shooting that line of neo-Christian cant . . . and you couldn't have got any closer to losing it.'

'True,' I admitted.

'I already know you're crazy,' she went on, 'but for the sake of my curiosity will you tell me whether you were really prepared to get shot? Did you really believe it, or were you handing him a line that went wrong?'

'On due reflection,' I answered, 'I haven't a clue. Ask Mariel. She may know whether I meant it or not, and what I meant if I did, but I don't.'

'You sure as hell weren't a neo-Christian before we came here,' she said. 'Or they'd never have let you on the ship.'

'As Pietrasante himself said to me,' I replied vaguely, 'it isn't illegal.'

'Just crazy.'

'Maybe.'

'It seems to me,' she commented, 'that you have so many beliefs they get more than a little tangled up.'

'Mixed motives,' I told her, 'are the best kind.'

'I suppose they'll raise a statue to you,' she said dryly.

'Right out there in the farmyard. The man who saved Floria. Twice. You reckon you really pulled it off back there, don't you? You think that because you were lucky at the crucial point you might have made Floria safe for pacifism forever?'

I shook my head. 'I don't think that at all. The rebellion has started ... it'll go on forever ... maybe just a little more slowly. But as Jason said ... what choice did I have? Yes or no. The same choice everybody has, every time. And it's always there, having to be taken again and again and again. I'll just take my choices, and the world – this world or any world – can take its own. My business is catching rats.'

'Coming from you,' she said, 'that's almost cynical.'

'I'm not a cynic,' I said. 'I'm a realist. Only cynics think there isn't any difference.'

I felt curiously self-satisfied as I rallied myself to think about it all. I suppose it was a sort of exultancy ... the sort you get when you find the fifth empty chamber in a game of Russian roulette. I wasn't really prepared to care anymore about what the hell I'd been playing at. I just wanted to get on to the next move.

I took hold of her hand, turned it right side up, and gave her back her souvenirs.

'You keep them,' I said. 'You need them more than I do.'

'Why?'

'To remind you that even if Goliath was the better man, David was luckier.'

'If David had stood still and let Goliath knock his head off,' she said, 'history might tell a different story.'

'As to that,' I pointed out, 'only time will tell. In the meantime, there are months of hard work in prospect. We have to identify the plasticity factor, and figure out a way to bring it under control – by force or persuasion or whatever damn way we can. It's not going to be easy.'

She clenched her fist around the metal pellets, and nodded absently. 'You know,' she said, 'it's strange that even here, where things looked to be so good and so healthy, and where the people have built a nation, there's still something lurking in the background which could destroy the whole thing.

When you think back to Kilner's reports, about the way every single hospitable, Earth-like world had discovered some way to be implacably hostile, you have to wonder whether there's more than luck involved. Maybe this whole scheme, the whole idea, is too ambitious. Maybe there never can be another human world.'

It was an uncharacteristically sober thought, for her. It revealed, perhaps for the first time, a depth of uncertainty underlying the glib carelessness.

But I had the answer.

'The gods are always against you,' I quoted. 'But sometimes you can cheat them.'

Robert Silverberg
THE SEED OF EARTH

The computer had chosen them – a small cross-section of humanity to serve Mankind's Destiny. Out of seven billion people on Earth mechanical chance had selected them as involuntary colonists on an unknown planet. In seven days they would be on their way, on a sink-or-swim mission to a lonely world beyond the limits of the Solar System.

It was a summons each had privately dreaded, yet always been prepared for. But no one had prepared them for the vicious attacks of sinister aliens . . .

Poul Anderson
THE
MAKESHIFT ROCKET

Knud Axel Syrup, chief engineer of the spaceship *Mercury Girl*, sat and drank his favourite beer and thought about the coming war he was so anxious to avoid. For Grendel – the planetoid on which he was stranded – had been occupied by a band of fiery Irish revolutionaries. And once the rival Anglians discovered this, their response would be speedy and violent.

Then, as Herr Syrup shook up a bottle of brew and let the foam shoot out of its top, he realized suddenly what could be done to get him off Grendel.

And so came about a marvellous spaceship – built of beer kegs, bound by gunk, upholstered with pretzel boxes, and powered by the mighty reaction forces of malted brew!